"The pony ride's a success, huh?"

Vicki turned to see Dan standing beside her. Everything inside her lurched when she saw he was in full uniform, gun on his hip. A tan deputy's uniform was different from the Austin PD's blue, but not different enough. It reminded her sharply that this man lived a life she wanted no part of ever again.

He'd been watching her little girl on the pony and smiling, but he looked at her when she didn't answer immediately.

"Yes," she said, finding her voice. "She's loving it. I can't thank you enough for all of this, including all the tickets. You didn't have to do that."

"No, I didn't. I wanted to. Some dreams just need to come true. Are you taking pictures? Because you'll never again see your four-year-old taking her first pony ride."

She nodded, feeling like she needed to catch her breath.

* * *

Conard County: The Next Generation!

Dear Reader,

Writing this book gave me a very warm feeling. I understand the traumas that life delivers, but I've also learned they can often be overcome through love and understanding. I have a great admiration for people who can rise from the ashes to take a risk again.

This book is particularly dear to me because I understand the difficulties of blended families, and any man who welcomes someone else's child into his heart as if she were his own is a hero to me. Vicki has a difficult road to travel as the widow of a cop, and her daughter, Krystal, is so young that being uprooted and moved creates additional problems. But deputy Dan Casey has had his own share of losses and has learned from them. With gentle patience he reaches out to Vicki and her daughter and brings them into a new bright world filled with love.

I hope you enjoy reading their story as much as I enjoyed writing it.

Rachel Lee

The Lawman Lassoes a Family

—

Rachel Lee

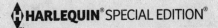
HARLEQUIN® SPECIAL EDITION®

Recycling programs
for this product may
not exist in your area.

ISBN-13: 978-0-373-65896-1

The Lawman Lassoes a Family

Printed in U.S.A.

www.Harlequin.com

Rachel Lee was hooked on writing by the age of twelve and practiced her craft as she moved from place to place all over the United States. This *New York Times* bestselling author now resides in Florida and has the joy of writing full-time.

Books by Rachel Lee

Harlequin Special Edition

Conard County: The Next Generation

A Conard County Baby
Reuniting with the Rancher
Thanksgiving Daddy
The Widow of Conard County

Montana Mavericks: 20 Years in the Saddle!

A Very Maverick Christmas

Harlequin Romantic Suspense

Conard County: The Next Generation

Guardian in Disguise
The Widow's Protector
Rancher's Deadly Risk
What She Saw
Rocky Mountain Lawman
Killer's Prey
Deadly Hunter
Snowstorm Confessions
Undercover Hunter

Visit the Author Profile page at Harlequin.com for more titles.

To all the stepparents who open their hearts.

Chapter One

On a warm summer afternoon, Conard County Sheriff's Deputy Dan Casey steered his truck around a rental truck half parked in Lena Winston's front yard, and then into his own driveway. Lena had been a friend for years, an older woman whose company he enjoyed. On Lena's porch he saw a little blonde girl, maybe four, sitting on the swing and rocking gently. She had her thumb in her mouth, a teddy bear in her arm and a sad look on her face.

Lena's niece, Vicki Templeton, must be moving in with her daughter. He looked at that van, not a very big one, but still wondered where they were going to put everything.

He was glad, though, that he'd had to leave his patrol unit at the garage for some work today. Climbing out of his car, he hurried inside to change into civvies before going to offer his help. Fewer reminders of cops might be welcome right now.

He knew from Lena that Vicki was a cop's widow, that she'd lost her husband a little over a year ago. Lena had stewed about it off and on for all this time, worried about her niece and grandniece, thinking it might be best for them to get away from reminders and come live with her.

Apparently, it had happened. As he wondered why Lena hadn't mentioned it would be so soon, he pulled on jeans and a black T-shirt blazoned with a wolf, and made his way next door. The little girl was still sitting on the swing. Female voices came from inside.

"Hi," he said from the yard, on the other side of the railing. "You must be Krystal. I'm Dan Casey. Are your mom and Aunt Lena inside?"

She took her thumb from her mouth and regarded him from eyes the color of the sky overhead. "I'm not supposed to suck my thumb."

"I didn't notice anything."

A shy smile curved her mouth, just a little. She pointed to his shirt. "That's not a dog."

"You're right, it's a wolf. A wolf from Yellowstone Park. Maybe you can see them one day."

Just then a young woman poked her head out the door. Blue eyes and black hair struck Dan immediately, as did a pretty face that looked tired almost beyond words.

"Krystal? Are you talking to someone?"

Krystal pointed and Dan moved closer to the steps. "Just me. Dan Casey. I live next door. Lena said you were moving in and I came to see if I can help. You must be Vicki."

The woman hesitated, then stepped out fully, brushing her hands on her jeans. "It's amazing how much dust seems to have moved with me." She wore a blue checked shirt with rolled-up sleeves, and tails knotted around her tiny waste. Her black hair had started to come loose from a ponytail set high on her head.

Dan stepped forward, reached up across the three steps to offer his hand. "It's a pleasure to meet you. Lena's been looking forward to this." Then he smiled. "Two fairly strong arms here, ready to pitch in. You can't turn me down."

She should have laughed, but all he saw was the flutter of a smile. "I think…"

Whatever she thought was lost as Lena came through the door behind her. Lena was in her midfifties, a little rounded by her years, with dark brown hair that was showing a lot of gray. Her eyes were a kindly brown. She, too, wore jeans and a man's tan work shirt.

"Dan! You arrived just in time. We got all the small stuff out, but now we've got Krystal's bed and some other big pieces. The three of us ought to be able to do it."

"I can call for more help if we need it," Dan assured her. "But where are you putting everything?"

Lena put her hands on her hips, a wry expression on her face. "That is a problem we'll deal with later."

Vicki looked at her aunt. "I could get rid of some of these things."

Lena shook her head firmly. "Nothing that's a comfort to Krystal or you is going anywhere. If we need room, I can easily get rid of some of my junk. God knows, most of it is far older than I am. Besides, you'll both sleep better in your own beds, and I like that sofa you brought. Never had a recliner before."

Dan paused. "You two moved a sofa?"

Lena laughed, a deep, throaty sound. "Not yet. I was waiting for you to get home."

He joined her laughter, but noticed that while Vicki smiled, she didn't laugh with them. Still grieving, he supposed, and now a huge move on top of everything. He felt genuine sympathy for her, and for the little girl, who looked utterly lost at the moment.

He wished he could gather them both in a hug, but knew the urge was ridiculous. He was a stranger to them, and he sure couldn't do anything to ease the pain of losing a husband and father.

He decided the best thing to do was focus on the moving.

"Let me see what's left in the truck," he said. "Then I'll know if I need to call for some help. And, Lena? Maybe you could show me where you want the big pieces?"

Dan called some friends, and soon there was a swirl of men moving from the truck into the house and back again. Vicki sort of got pushed to one side as Lena supervised the unloading. Occasionally her aunt questioned her about where she wanted something, but mostly Vicki just sat with Krystal curled against her side, and watched the activity.

Had she really brought so much with her? Apparently so. She felt a twinge of guilt for dumping so much on her aunt, but she'd spent a great deal of time beforehand selling things and giving them away.

Yet she had to bring things that were important to

Krystal, or that would become important to her later. Her father's awards. All the photographs. Her toys. Krystal had been allowed to help with the decisions, and made it clear what was to come with them.

Nor was Vicki entirely blameless. There were some items she just couldn't let go of, either. Memories of Hal had attached themselves everywhere, and parting with some of them had been downright painful.

Maybe she should have put stuff in a storage room, but she had discovered she wasn't ready to make that big a break yet herself. Struggling to move forward with her life had meant moving to a new place, away from the constant attentions of Hal's colleagues and their spouses, who had gone out of their way to make sure she always had someone available, that she was left out of nothing they did. Even Krystal had been included in their caring, as various people from the department took her on outings, or just made themselves available.

At some point it had hit her: she could continue to live as Hal's widow, surrounded by his well-meaning friends, which made it impossible for her to move on. Or she could take her aunt's repeated offers and just do it.

Vicki hoped she hadn't made the biggest mistake of her life.

She worried about Krystal, who seemed to be adjusting to her father's absence, but didn't appear to understand he would never come home. Vicki worried that this move might stress the girl even more. Now she had lost every single thing that was familiar except for what they had brought with them.

Maybe Vicki's decision had been selfish.

"Mommy?"

"Yes, honey?"

"I sucked my thumb. The man saw me."

Vicki felt her eyes prickle with tears she couldn't allow herself to shed. Gathering her daughter onto her lap, she hugged her tight. "That's okay, honey. When you're ready to stop doing it, you will."

Krystal had stopped sucking her thumb by eighteen months of age. The habit had returned within days of her father's death. Vicki wasn't going to give her a hard time about comforting herself.

"But I'm a big girl," Krys said. "Big girls don't suck their thumbs."

"Who told you that?"

"Jenny."

Jenny had been a friend at preschool. "Well, that's not always true, Krys. Some grown-ups still do it."

Krystal stirred and looked up. "So I'm still a big girl?"

"You're a wonderful big girl."

"Aunt Lena's house smells funny."

"She uses sachets. We'll get used to it."

Krystal sighed, closed her eyes and melted into Vicki. A precious moment.

Vicki's gaze strayed to the men who were unloading her life, and saw they were about finished. She knew Dan Casey was a deputy, because Lena had mentioned him occasionally over the years. A good neighbor, Lena had judged him.

He was certainly being a good neighbor now. Vicki watched him and three other men carry the recliner sofa across the ramp and into the house. A good-looking man, maybe getting near forty, although she couldn't be sure. He definitely looked older than Hal, and Hal had been thirty-three, just a year older than Vicki.

Cops, she thought. Hal's friends had helped her load, and now Dan and his friends were helping unload. No escape, but at least these cops hadn't been her husband's friends.

Suddenly she realized he was looking at her. Dark hair, gray eyes, very fit. He stepped over.

"Well," he said, "Lena's house is packed. We'll be back to move some stuff to her basement or garage once she makes up her mind what she wants to do with it. But listen, I'm going out to get dinner for everyone. Is there anything Krystal doesn't like to eat?"

"She's not picky." Not anymore. She'd outgrown that stage a while back.

"Then what about you? What would you like her to eat?"

Krystal stirred. "I want a hamburger." As clear as a bell.

Dan looked at Vicki, who nodded. Then he squatted and smiled at Krystal. "A hamburger just for you. What do you want on it?"

"Ketchup. I hate pickles."

"You got it. Vicki?"

"Whatever you all want is fine by me. Thank you."

He nodded and straightened. The ramp was being shoved back into the truck, the rear doors closed and locked. Then they parked the truck on the street behind her little car, still sitting on the towing trailer.

It was done, Vicki thought. She'd broken with her past. She just hoped she hadn't broken her daughter in the process.

* * *

Before Dan returned with food, the other men headed home, explaining they had families, but promising to come back when needed. Vicki could feel the blue wall enclosing her in its comforting grip already. What had she thought she was escaping? But she knew: familiar faces that inevitably reminded her of her loss. At least these were all new faces, with no connection to Hal.

She was still sitting on the porch with Krystal in her lap when Dan returned carrying big brown bags.

"Dinner bell," he said cheerfully. "And one big hamburger for Miss Krystal here."

The words galvanized Krystal for the first time in hours. She squirmed off Vicki's lamp, left her teddy bear behind and excitedly followed Dan into the house.

Vicki followed more reluctantly. Tired as she was from the long drive and unloading, not to mention getting ready for this big move, she hadn't felt hungry for a while. She ate only because she had to, not because she wanted to. It was like the period right after the shock of Hal's death.

Maybe this move had been a bad idea for a whole lot of reasons.

Lena had a big house, as local houses went, but right now it was full of boxes and excess furniture. The dining room was still clear, though, and they ate there at a table that showed the effects of the years, with scratches, faded stains and a few deep dings.

Lena brought out plates and flatware, but Krystal wanted to eat from the foam box. Her burger was huge, so Vicki cut it in half for her, and tried not to look at the mound of french fries. Of course, Krys went first for the fries, a rare treat.

Two of the containers held huge salads, so Vicki put some in a bowl next to Krys. "Eat your salad, too, honey."

"I will."

Lena spoke. "Sit down and eat, Vicki. You're exhausted. I can look after Krys's needs, can't I, hon?"

Krys nodded. Whatever else might be going on inside her, her appetite hadn't diminished.

Vicki took a seat at last, with Krystal between her and Lena, and Dan across the way.

"You must be tired," he said to her. He still hadn't opened the box in front of him. "I can just take my meal and run."

Considering how he had helped, and that he'd run out to get this meal for them, letting him leave would be churlish, no matter how fatigued she was feeling.

"No, please," she said. "You've been so kind to us today. I'm tired, but not that tired." She tried for a smile and apparently managed it, because he returned it with one of his own.

"Mommy worked hard," Krystal announced, at last reaching for her burger. "I had to stay with friends lotsa times."

"Yes you did, honey. But you helped me choose, didn't you?"

Krys nodded, then disappeared behind the huge burger. She wouldn't be able to get her mouth around it, a mess would ensue and Vicki didn't care. She was just glad to see Krys enjoying herself.

Vicki looked at Lena. "We took over your house. I'm sorry."

"And I'm not," her aunt said. "This is a big house for one woman." She looked at Dan. "I don't know if I ever told you, but this is the family house, from the earliest days of Conard City. It's been passed down for nearly a hundred years, and here I am, rambling around in a house that was meant for a big family. There's plenty of room for two more. We just need to do some sorting and arranging. I might not have it all settled by tomorrow, though."

"Probably not," Dan agreed, holding half a sandwich in his hand. "Just let me know when you want help and how much you need. But take your time." He glanced toward the front room with a humorous twinkle in his eyes. "That's a lot of boxes, never mind furniture."

"I probably overdid it," Vicki said. "Maybe I just gave up. Sorting, selling things, giving them away..." She looked down. "I guess I just couldn't do it anymore."

Lena reached out and patted her hand. "You did just fine. I wasn't kidding, Vicki. I didn't want either of you to give up a single thing that you want. It's not necessary. As for some of the old stuff around here, I'll be glad to have a reason to see the last of it." She laughed and reached for her bowl of salad. "You know, more than once I've had a fantasy about bringing in a decorator to do the whole place over. Beyond my means, I know, but I'm not going to mind the changes." Then she leaned over and looked at Krystal. "And you, my dear Krys, have a whole room for a playroom. Or you will once we move a few things out."

"Goodie," said Krystal, her mouth full of hamburger. Vicki let it go.

"Should I groan now?" Dan asked. Lena laughed.

Vicki kept her eyes down, even as she tried to smile. It was impossible not to look at Dan and see the spark of male interest in his gaze. She wasn't ready for that, didn't know if she would ever be, but she was absolutely determined never again to care for a cop. One trip through that hell had been enough for a lifetime.

Right now she had only one concern, helping Krys through another major upheaval. Vicki hoped it would be the last one, but she wasn't going to throw anything else into the pot for the girl. Now her daughter had not only lost her father, but she'd lost everything familiar except what they could carry with them. All her friends, her preschool, the places they'd frequented. Ripped away from her.

Vicki barely heard the rest of the conversation as she once again debated with herself the wisdom of her decision. She knew she needed to move on, both for her own sake and her daughter's. She had to build them a life of some sort away from the haunting memories. She had to set an example of strength, find some joy in life again.

So yes, she'd had good reasons for this move. But gazing at Krystal, who was beginning to look as if dinner had made her sleepy, she wondered whose interests had driven her more.

"Honey? Are you getting sleepy?"

Krys lifted her head, trying to look alert, but failing. "I guess. Read me a story?"

"You bet."

"Just take her up," Lena said. "I'll clean up. We can reheat her burger for her lunch tomorrow."

Upstairs, Vicki found the box with Krys's sheets and pillows, and soon the bed looked familiar again, with

brightly colored balloons on the linens and comforter.
Krys climbed in after allowing her mother to wash her
face and hands at the bathroom sink, then waited ex-
pectantly for her story.

She wasn't going to last long, Vicki thought as she
dug out one of her daughter's favorite Dr. Seuss stories.
The Boston rocker had made it up here, so she pulled
it over to the bed and held Krys's hand while she read
the silly, hypnotic words.

Krys's eyes started to close, but Vicki kept reading
so that the happy rhymes would follow her into sleep.
Soon, though, the girl seemed fast asleep, her breath-
ing deep and regular. Vicki eased her hand away and
stood, placing the book on the chair.

The floor creaked a little as she crossed tiptoe to
the door, and Krys's voice stopped her.

"Mommy? Don't go away like Daddy did."

The words froze Vicki like an electric shock. Anguish she had believed was lessening seized her in a
painful grip, twisting her heart until she wanted to cry
out from it. She squeezed her eyes shut briefly, then
turned, knowing she had to answer her daughter.

But Krys had already fallen back asleep. A little
murmur escaped her and she rolled on her side, hugging her pillow.

Vicki crept out. At the top of the stairs she sagged
until she sat on a riser, and let hot, silent tears fall.

"Your grandniece is cute as a button," Dan said as
he helped clear the table. Lena put on some coffee and
invited him to stay.

"She certainly is," Lena agreed. "Now stay for a few

minutes, Dan. I know how you love your coffee, and it's the least I can do after all your help."

"Any neighbor would have helped," he said dismissively. "Glad to do it."

"Stay anyway. What are you going to do? Head home and sprawl in front of the TV with some soccer game?"

Dan laughed. "You have me pegged."

Lena arched a brow at him. "Yeah. As a man who works hard and wants to relax when he gets home. Instead you moved half a house."

He shook his head. "Don't make too much of it, Lena. I had an easy day and the workout felt good. As for sprawling in front of the TV, I do less of that than you think."

She laughed. "Maybe so. I don't exactly keep an eye on you."

"Thank goodness. My reputation probably wouldn't survive it."

They carried their coffee into the front room. "That's a really nice couch," he remarked. He'd like one himself, a dual recliner such as that. But he didn't sit on it. He wasn't a dullard, and he was willing to bet one end or the other had been Vicki's husband's seat. Dan didn't want her to see him on it when she came back down.

He picked his way to Lena's old sofa and took his usual place on it. She often invited him over for dinner or dessert, especially when he did some little thing for her around the place that she couldn't do herself. And Lena could do quite a lot herself, so it wasn't as if she imposed.

Boxes, shoved to the side, made the room feel tiny, which it never had before.

"How much are you planning to get rid of?" he asked. This house had been the same the whole time he'd known Lena, and even in its current jumbled state he could see the place he knew. He wondered if she was going to find it more difficult than she was letting on.

Lena waved a hand. "As much as I need to. Probably won't be as much as it looks like right now. Everything I have are hand-me-downs. I never got a chance to do this place the way I wanted, except for some curtains and small things. I feel like the caretaker of a museum sometimes. The Winston Family Museum. There are a number of things I'm attached to, but most of it is just here. No history, no old memories, no meaning."

"I don't know whether to say that's good or that's sad."

"Both," she said wryly. "Vicki gets it next. It might as well be more to her liking."

Dan leaned forward, holding his mug between both hands as he rested his elbows on his knees. "Hey, you've got a lot of good years left. Don't be talking like that."

"Like what? I'm almost fifty-five, young by the reckoning of most. I might have another thirty years. Then again, I could slip on ice this next winter and be done. You never know, Dan."

"No." This conversation was taking a maudlin turn, and he wondered if it had to do with Vicki. Not that she had started it, but maybe what had happened to her niece had caused Lena to start thinking about these things. He sought another avenue.

"So Vicki is your sister's daughter? I know you told me, but I've never had the instincts of a genealogist."

Lena barked a laugh. "That's right. She took off out

of here when she was eighteen, and never came back. I used to go visit her, the way I went to visit Vicki."

He began to remember stories from over the years. Shortly after Vicki had graduated from college, Lena's sister had died. Vicki's father had apparently vanished from the scene before she was born. "Lou, wasn't it? Your sister? Skydiving accident?"

Lena smiled faintly. "Live it while you have it, that's my motto. I just chose a less risky way of life. Lou, on the other hand, had a whole bucket list of wild things she wanted to do once Vicki was old enough."

Dan hesitated, but for some reason he wanted a clear picture of the situation. Maybe it was just the cop in him. "And no family on Vicki's husband's side?"

"Hal grew up in foster care. Near as I could tell, he felt closer to the Police Athletic League than any of his foster families, and there were a lot of them."

"So that leaves you."

"It sure does. And since I was never blessed with a family of my own, I'm considering myself blessed right now."

Dan grinned. "I don't get why you weren't snapped up."

Lena arched a brow. "Oh, there were snappers. I just kept throwing them back in the river."

He unleashed a belly laugh. "I love you, Lena."

She rolled her eyes. "Just not like that. I get it." Then she joined his laughter.

Upstairs, Vicki heard the laughter and decided that she needed to go down. After all, she'd made this move, wrenching her daughter away from the only home she'd ever known, so they could start fresh. That meant she had to rejoin the world again.

She stopped in the bathroom, wiped away the tears and applied cold water to her eyes. After a couple minutes, she realized that she couldn't erase the puffiness. They were going to know she had been weeping.

Oh, well. She'd do it again countless times. Grief was nothing to be ashamed of, and if it made Dan uneasy…well, he didn't have to stay. She took a brush to her hair, smoothing it back into a neat ponytail, then stiffened herself to face the world.

She entered the living room and found Lena sitting on a rocker and Dan sitting on the old couch. Habit led her to take her usual end of the recliner sofa, where she curled her legs under her.

"Want some coffee?" Vicki asked. "Just made a pot."

"I'll get it. Thanks, Lena."

Her aunt stood. "Stay right there. I'm not the one who spent weeks moving. Be right back."

Which left her alone with Dan. He sat with his legs splayed, the mug cradled in both hands, his elbows resting on his thighs.

"How long did you drive today?" he asked. "Austin's quite a piece."

"We broke it up. There's just so long you can keep a four-year-old cooped up in a vehicle. We left Laramie this morning."

"Not too bad, then."

"No." Which kind of ended the conversation. She wanted to sigh as she realized that she'd lost the basic skill of making small talk. Over the past year, her friends and Hal's had taken up all the slack on that front, leaving her to join in when she felt like it. She hadn't filled any gaps or silences.

"Your daughter is cute," Dan said after a pause. "Adorable. Is she really attached to that teddy bear?"

"Off and on. Not like when she was a baby and she needed a particular blanket or stuffed animal. During the trip, the bear was handy." At least Vicki had managed more than a single word.

God, she felt so out of place and out of sync. All the weeks of preparation, the long drive, and now she had arrived, and felt as if she'd been cast adrift.

"You ever been here before?" he asked. "I don't remember seeing you, but I only moved in next door three years ago."

Lena returned with a mug for Vicki, and the coffeepot to pour fresh for everyone. "Never visited me," she remarked. "No, I had to fly to Austin to see her." She placed the pot on an old table and returned to her rocker.

Vicki wondered if she should apologize. Her head was swimming, trying to order things, make sense of everything, and she had no idea what she should say.

"Not that I wanted it any other way," Lena said, her eyes twinkling. "I got to travel the world. Well, Texas, anyway. I even got to meet the oversize Texas ego."

Helplessly, Vicki felt a small laugh escape her. "It's a state of mind, you know."

"I noticed," Lena said tartly. "Now, I'm not saying they don't have a lot to be proud of, but if you ask me, it was really something back there for a while when Texans who'd moved away sent for bags of Texas dirt to put under delivery tables so their babies could be born on Texas soil. And the state issued honorary birth certificates."

Dan appeared astonished. "For real?"

"Unless I misread the story." Lena looked at Vicki. "Are they still doing that?"

"I have no idea, honestly. I thought it was just a brief fad when it occurred, and I'm positive the state isn't in the business of giving honorary birth certificates."

Lena chuckled. "Well, of course it would turn out to be a Texas-sized story."

"It's a good one, though." Dan smiled. "It probably even grew legs for a while."

"It grew legs for me," Lena said. "Now I'm wondering how many times I told that story. I may have a lot of apologizing to do."

"Don't bother," said Dan. "It's a good yarn, and apparently at least a few people must have sent for Texas dirt."

"That much was true," Vicki said. "A few people. Maybe occasionally someone still does it, but only for their own amusement. It doesn't make a real difference as far as I know."

Silence fell for a few minutes. Vicki felt uneasy. Surely she ought to have something else to contribute?

Then Dan spoke again. "I think you'll like living here. It's a pretty good town, as small towns go. People are friendly. We can't keep up with a place like Austin for excitement and entertainment, but we have other advantages."

He rose, putting aside his mug. "I'm going to go now, Lena. Vicki looks exhausted, and we all have a lot to do tomorrow." He paused in front of Vicki. "I'm glad I finally got to meet you."

Then he was gone, leaving the two women sitting in silence.

"Did Krys go to sleep okay?" Lena eventually asked.

"Out like a light."

"Then I suggest you do the same, my girl. You're starting to look pale. Need help making up your bed?"

"Only if I can't find the sheets."

Lena laughed. "I got spares if you need them. Let's go and settle you."

Vicki wondered if she'd ever feel settled again, then made up her mind that she would. Compared to the past year, this was a small challenge. Feeling better, she followed her aunt upstairs.

Chapter Two

Lena was the bookkeeper for Freitag's Mercantile. She often joked that there was little as boring in the world as a bookkeeper, unless it was a CPA. Vicki, who found her aunt anything but dull, always smiled or laughed, but she didn't believe it. Besides, boring jobs sounded awfully good these days. For her part, until Hal's death, she'd taught kindergarten, but there wasn't a job available here yet.

Which was fine, she told herself as she fed Krys her breakfast, after Lena departed for a half day. Vicki wanted to spend as much time as possible with Krys, until the girl was truly settled here. In the meantime, Vicki had plenty in savings from insurance and death benefits, plus the money she and Hal had been saving toward a house. She could get by for years if necessary.

She had to deal with the present. Sitting at the table

with Krys, who looked a lot perkier today, she said, "How about we set up your bedroom and playroom this morning?"

Krys tilted her head, her blue eyes bright. "Okay. I can tell you where to put everything?"

"Most of it, anyway. We'll have to see how things fit."

"Aunt Lena has lots of stuff."

Vicki nodded guiltily. Lena had assured her there was ample room, and in terms of space, there was. The problem was that this house had accumulated so much over the years that the space was pretty full. With her additions, it was packed.

"We may not be able to get everything just right," she told her daughter. "We'll have to see where there's room."

Krys nodded and emptied her bowl by drinking the last of the milk from it. Vicki reached over with her napkin to wipe away a milky mustache and a few dribbles.

"Are there kids here?" her daughter asked as they headed upstairs.

"Plenty, I'm sure. Once we get some unpacking done, we'll go look for some."

"'Kay. I liked that man. He's coming back, right?"

"Yes, to help with moving." Dan Casey, another cop. Didn't it just figure? And even in her dulled state, Vicki had noticed how attractive he was. Well, that was best buried immediately. No more cops ever, and moving on didn't mean she was ready to dive into some relationship, anyway.

Time. She needed more time. Whoever had decided

that a year was enough time for mourning evidently had never really mourned.

She pushed aside her mood and focused on enjoying Krys's excitement. For the little girl, opening boxes and rediscovering treasures that had been steadily packed away over the past few weeks seemed to be almost like Christmas morning. Every rediscovered belonging, no matter how old or familiar, was greeted as if it were brand-new.

The child's excitement was contagious, and Vicki joined in wholeheartedly. The bedroom was relatively easy. Lena had gotten rid of everything except a decent chest of drawers, and with Krys's bed and the Boston rocker, all they needed to do was unpack clothes and books, and some of the stuffed animals Krys wanted in the room with her.

The playroom turned into a bigger challenge. It already contained a narrow bed, a chest and a bureau. Vicki moved the bed over against the wall, thinking that she could probably cover it with pillows and a spread, and turn it into a daybed. Krys slowed down a little, having to decide where each and every toy should go.

Vicki didn't rush her. They weren't going anywhere soon, and the child might as well enjoy whatever control she could over a life that had changed so drastically.

It amazed Vicki anew the number of toys Krys had, even though she herself had packed them. She and Hal had tried never to overindulge their daughter, but during the past year that had gone out the window. So often one of Hal's colleagues would stop by bearing a gift. It was well-meant, but now Krys had way too many toys.

But she had refused to part with a single one, and Vicki hadn't had the heart to disagree with her. Krys had lost too much, the move was a huge change, and if she needed every one of those toys for comfort, then they came along.

By noon, when Lena returned, they were only halfway through the unpacking, and Vicki suspected that Krys was dawdling a little. Getting tired or getting overwhelmed? She couldn't really tell, and the child didn't have the self-awareness yet to define why she was slowing down.

"Lunchtime," Lena called up from the foot of the stairs.

Krys seemed glad of the break and hurried down. Vicki took a little longer, freshening a bit in the bathroom and wishing she had a window into her daughter's head. Even teaching kindergarten, she sometimes found youngsters this age to be inscrutable mysteries. You could tell when something was wrong, but you couldn't always find out what the problem was.

Krys wanted her leftover hamburger, and seemed to enjoy it even after a trip through the microwave. Lena and Vicki ate ham on rye.

"Dan called this morning. He got a half day, too, and should be over soon. I guess I need to figure out what I want moved where."

"Lena…"

Her aunt shook her head. "No. Don't say it. I made most of the decisions already, once you agreed to come. Vicki, believe me, I wouldn't have kept pestering you to come here if I thought it was going to be inconvenient."

"But—"

"Hush. We're both going to do some adapting. It's not a major crisis."

Vicki wasn't entirely certain about that, but decided to let it go unless a crisis blew up on its own.

When Dan arrived, Vicki and Krystal were pretty much relegated to the front porch swing. Lena wanted to label items that needed to be moved according to where she wanted them, and Dan accompanied her, taking notes to determine how much help he'd need.

"I could hire some people," Vicki said at one point.

Dan merely gave her a wry look. "Don't offend me."

How was she supposed to take that? All she knew was that a big handsome man was moving in on her life. Her attraction to him made her feel a bit uneasy, and she quickly squashed it. Krystal yawned and curled up on the swing with her head in her mother's lap. That effectively put Vicki out of the action.

It was a perfect day, however. A gentle breeze blew, and the temperature was somewhere in the midseventies. For a Texan it felt like spring, but this was summer in Wyoming. With her hand resting on Krystal's shoulder, Vicki pushed the swing gently and decided to accept her exile from all the doings inside.

It was Lena's house, and it would be handled Lena's way.

It was nearly four when Dan emerged and went around the corner to the garage. He returned a few minutes later with two folding lawn chairs and set them on the porch. Lena appeared a little while later with a pitcher of lemonade and glasses full of ice on a tray. Krystal barely stirred. Evidently she was worn-out, whether from all the activity earlier, from the trip or from the changes, Vicki couldn't guess. She let her daughter sleep on.

"Okay," said Lena. "That's half the battle done."

"Which half?" asked Vicki.

"Everything's labeled that I want gone. Some for basement storage, but a lot for the garage." She grinned. "I'm going to have a big garage sale. Gawd, I've wanted to do that for so long."

Dan laughed quietly. "You should have told me."

"I dither sometimes. Like I said, this place feels like the Winston Family Museum. Anyway, Vicki, I want you to go through. If you see any furniture I've labeled that you like, then let me know. I want the house to please you, too."

Vicki opened her mouth, then snapped it closed.

Dan flashed her an attractive grin. "Don't argue with Lena. There's no winning."

"I'm beginning to realize that."

He glanced out toward the street. "We need to turn in that rental truck and get your car off the tow trolley."

"There's supposed to be someplace here in town," Vicki said.

"On the west side. I can show you."

At that moment, Krystal sat up. The instant she saw Dan, her face lit up.

Vicki felt her heart sink. This could turn out to be bad. Another cop. Damn, why couldn't she escape cops?

"Go deal with it," Lena said. "Krystal can help me with a few things after she finishes her lemonade."

Krystal beamed.

While Vicki went inside the rental place to turn in the vehicle, Dan unhooked her car and rolled it off the trolley. It took him only a minute to reconnect her lights properly, then he leaned against the side of the truck to wait for her.

He had the distinct impression he was pushing himself into territory where he wasn't wanted. Why, he didn't know. It was something in Vicki's demeanor. Not that it really mattered. He wasn't going to stop helping Lena, and even if Vicki didn't want him around, he felt a duty to Krystal. That girl's daddy had been a cop, and he felt obligated to at least keep an eye on her and step up where he could.

If Vicki would allow him to.

He folded his arms and crossed his legs at the ankles, letting the afternoon sun bathe him with warmth. He knew a little about grieving. He'd lost his wife to cancer five years ago, and he still sometimes missed her so much he wondered if he could stand it. That might be what he was sensing in Vicki.

It had been only a little more than a year for her. A year was an infinity in terms of pain, but short in terms of recovering. The woman was probably a walking raw nerve ending.

He still wondered at her decision to come here. Oh, he'd been listening to Lena suggest it for months now, and knew it was what his neighbor had hoped for, but what about Vicki? She had left behind her support network, her friends, her home. And so had Krystal. Why? He'd never felt the least desire to leave Conard City after Callie's death. Yeah, he'd eventually bought a house, but that hadn't deprived him of anything. He and Callie had been living in one of the apartments near the college, and they'd always planned to buy their own place. He'd felt as if he was fulfilling the dream for both of them.

But it was entirely different for Vicki. And for Krystal. He kept coming back to that little girl and wondering if this were best for *her*. Of course, Vicki was her mother and must have had her reasons, must have determined this complete severing would benefit her in the long run.

Maybe it would. Krystal had been three when her daddy died. She probably hardly remembered him. She wouldn't remember all that much about being four, either. Dan sure couldn't. But she *would* remember this move.

At least he didn't have a kid to worry about, so those were shoes that didn't fit him even temporarily. He and Callie had wanted kids, though. When they found out why they couldn't, it had been too late for Callie.

Hell. He uncrossed his ankles, straightened and scuffed his foot at the dirt. He didn't want to run down this road again, but Vicki's situation was reminding him. Funny how he thought he'd moved on, until something reared up to remind him he hadn't moved as far as he thought he had.

The smart thing to do might just be to stay away, unless Lena needed him. Keep his hard-won equilibrium in place. But then he thought of Krystal, a cop's little girl, and Vicki, a cop's widow, and he knew it wasn't in him to stay away.

A decent human being would help however he could. But for a cop it went beyond that. The family took care of its own, and Vicki and her daughter were family.

Simplistic, maybe, but every cop counted on that

kind of support for his or her family when something bad happened.

He looked up at the sound of footsteps, and saw Vicki approaching from the office. Today she wore jeans again, but this time with a T-shirt emblazoned with the Alamo. Texan through and through, he thought, smiling faintly.

The smile she gave him looked brittle. "All done."

He gestured to the car. "All ready."

"Thanks."

He hesitated a beat, then said, "I can walk back, if you like."

Her expression turned quizzical. "Why should you do that?"

"You might be feeling a little overwhelmed."

Her blue eyes widened a shade, then she shook her head. "Hop in, cowboy. I'm going to feel overwhelmed for a while."

So he climbed into her little Toyota while she started the engine. It was a tight fit, but he didn't want to push the seat back. Adjusting the car for himself struck him as an intrusion.

"Give yourself some leg room," she said as she turned the car and drove toward the street.

She was observant. Reaching for the lever, he pushed the seat back. He sought a way into conversation that wouldn't come out wrong. "Is this a big adventure for Krystal?"

"So far she seems to be reacting that way. This morning was like Christmas as she was unpacking her toys. And I need to find her some friends soon."

"There's a park just a couple blocks from the house.

Swings, monkey bars, slides, sandbox. That might be a good starting point."

"Thanks. I'll take her there."

Okay, then. As a cop he had become fairly good at hearing what wasn't said. She hadn't asked him to show her the park. She didn't want him to. Vicki Templeton was setting boundaries wherever she could.

Fine by him. There was a difference between being there if she needed anything, and pushing himself on her. He could do the former, and it might be better in the long run. He had some rawness himself since Callie and hadn't even dated since her death. Eventually, he supposed he would again, but he'd know when the time was right. For now, however, he couldn't imagine anyone in Callie's place.

Deciding that Vicki might be wise, he settled back, intending to focus solely on helping Lena clear her house.

And on Krystal. Vicki might think it was a big adventure for the child, but he'd seen her sitting on a porch swing, sucking her thumb and looking like an abandoned, weary waif.

He would do everything he could for that child. Starting with finding her a friend.

"Where's Dan?" Lena asked, when Vicki stepped inside.

"He said he had something to do, and would see you tomorrow." From upstairs, she could hear Krys singing at the top of her lungs. Vicki looked up. "She sounds happy."

"For now. I left her to finish her playroom. There

wasn't much left to do, and she's pretty certain about where she wants everything."

"She sure is." Vicki dropped her purse on the hall table. "I told her to put her toys where she wanted in there. I hope it was okay."

"Perfectly okay." Lena slipped her arm around Vicki's shoulders. "Now let's you and me have a quiet cup of coffee and relax for a minute. You've earned a chance to take a deep breath."

Vicki hesitated only briefly. Keeping busy had become a kind of refuge for her, a way to keep grief and despair at bay. Coming here had been a way to escape the constant reminders of loss. Somehow it just hadn't been getting easier.

Lena took them into her kitchen, which like many older ones didn't have a lot of cabinetry or counter space, but instead had a big round table for most kitchen chores. Despite its lack of the conveniences Vicki expected, it was a large room and probably worked well. One long bank of counters and cabinets provided enough room for a microwave and a food processor, and little else. A sink with a short counter filled a second wall. That left a stove and refrigerator side by side on the third wall, and the table, which sat beneath the wide windows.

The coffee had already brewed and Lena set out two mugs for them. Vicki slid into an old oak chair at the table, saying, "We must seem like an invasion force to you."

Lena laughed. "Actually, no. Why do you think I kept asking you to come here? This is a big old house, too big for one person, and it's going to be yours someday, anyway. You might as well make any changes you want. Better than being caretaker of the family museum."

Vicki laughed helplessly. "You've said that before. Do you really feel that way?"

"Sometimes, yes." Lena sat near her. "When your grandparents were alive, that was one thing. The three of us got along pretty well, and the place was…well, what it was. But it's been a while since they passed. This place echoes with just me, and I keep getting an itch to change it somehow. It always seemed like a ridiculous expense just for me. But now there's you and Krystal, and I think changing this house around is going to be good for me. For all of us."

"I hope so."

Lena regarded her thoughtfully. "Does something about Dan bother you?"

Vicki started. "No. Why?"

"I know he's a cop and you were trying to get away from being smothered by them, but he's not like that."

"No?" She waited, tensing.

"No. He's a widower, you know."

Vicki felt her heart jump uncomfortably. "He is?"

"Yup. Lost his wife to ovarian cancer a bit over five years ago. I knew her, too. Small town. Anyway, he's become a good friend of mine, and I'd hate for you to feel uncomfortable with him."

Vicki nodded and realized that she had indeed felt a resistance toward him. Not because of him; he hadn't done one thing to make her feel that way. But because she feared…what, exactly? He might be a cop, but he wasn't a reminder. She shifted uncomfortably. "I'm sorry, Lena."

"No need. You and I have been talking frequently

since Hal died. I think I have some understanding of the problems you've been dealing with. It might give you some comfort to know Dan's been through a lot of it, too. Anyway, he's a good friend. He could be your friend, as well, but he doesn't have to be. I just want you to know that he is *my* friend."

Now Vicki felt just awful. She must have done something to cause her aunt to speak this way. "I don't want to make him feel unwelcome."

"I'm sure you don't. And you've been dealing with a lot. I only brought it up because…well, he was supposed to come here for dinner tonight. I expected him to return with you. Did something happen?"

"Not a thing. He was very helpful, and he told me about the park where I could take Krys."

"Well, then, I'm going to call that young man and find out what's going on."

If she hadn't felt so bad, Vicki might have laughed. Dan was young enough, but Vicki wasn't so old that she should be thinking of him as "that young man."

Lena went to the wall phone and called Dan. "I hear you're skipping out on dinner. You never pass on my fried chicken."

Vicki gestured that she was going to the bathroom, then slipped out. It seemed she couldn't escape Dan, but then she wondered why she should even want to. He'd been pleasant and helpful, and he had no ties with her past, other than Lena. What was going on inside her?

She wondered if she would ever get herself sorted out.

"Mommy?"

She looked up and saw Krystal at the head of the stairs. "Yes, sweetie?"

"I finished. Come see."

Vicki climbed the stairs to join her daughter in her new playroom. "I heard you singing when I came home. It sounded like you were having fun."

"Aunt Lena said I could do it myself. I'm a big girl now."

That was the second time in two days. When she reached the top of the stairs, Vicki stroked her daughter's blond head and wondered if she had somehow put pressure on the child, making her feel she needed to grow up faster. Even with all her experience with children, Vicki didn't know. They all seemed to want to grow up fast. But sometimes they had reasons that were darker than their years should justify.

The organization in the room existed only in her daughter's eyes, but Vicki praised it sincerely. This was one place Krystal could express herself and control her environment, and not for the world would Vicki take that away from her.

Then she saw a photograph on the shelf and felt gut-punched. It was a family photo of her, Hal and Krys, taken on Krys's third birthday. Balloons decorated the background, and all three of them were beaming.

Vicki hesitated, then said, "I thought you liked that picture by your bed."

Krys shook her head. "I can't see him when I sleep."

"Oh. I didn't think of that." The giant fist, so familiar over the past year, once again reached out and grabbed Vicki's heart, squeezing it until she almost couldn't breathe. Her knees weakened and she sat on the edge of the bed, which had almost disappeared beneath stuffed animals.

Krystal climbed up beside her. "See?"

Indeed, she could see. Krystal had found the place in the room where Hal's photo could see her everywhere. His dark, smiling eyes seemed to be looking at them right now.

"Daddy likes it here," she announced. "Tell me about my party again?"

Despite feeling as if her chest were being crushed, Vicki told the familiar story of Krystal's third birthday party. It had become a ritual, and if she skipped even one word, Krys reminded her.

Hugging her daughter, she forced life into her voice, when she felt as if she had no life left.

Dinner with Dan had been a pleasant time. They ate at the big dining room table again with the overhead chandelier adding some cheer. He and Lena spoke about doings around the county, and Dan included Krystal as often as possible, asking her about her new playroom, but in no way pushing any boundaries.

By the time Vicki took her daughter upstairs for a bath and bed, she felt more comfortable with the whole idea of Dan being around frequently. Unlike some of Hal's friends, he wasn't trying to play the father role for the girl. He just treated her as if she were another friend at the table.

Later, when she went back downstairs, he was still here, chatting with Lena in the living room. Vicki wished she could enjoy the kind of comfortable friendship they seemed to, and knew she was the only one holding back.

It was always possible she might not like him as much as Lena did, but she'd never know unless she joined the two of them.

Lena had made it clear that they were friends, and that wasn't going to change. Vicki still wasn't sure what she had done that had made Dan originally decide not to come for dinner, but she resolved to be friendlier.

If she could figure out how. She seemed to have become somewhat socially inept after the past year. But of course, she'd stopped meeting new people and had become enclosed by the blue wall of Hank's friends. If she sat for hours without speaking, they didn't worry about it. They just included her, then let her be.

Despite the passage of time, she'd seemed to want to be left alone more rather than less. It was part of what had driven her to accept Lena's invitation—the feeling that Hal's friends, despite their best intentions, were holding her in some kind of stasis. That with them she would always be Hal's widow.

Well, if she was to have any life at all other than being his widow and Krystal's mom, now was the time to start. And friendship was a good place to begin.

She went to the kitchen to pour herself coffee before joining them. Once again, she found Dan and her aunt on Lena's old couch. Vicki wondered if her recliner sofa was radioactive or something.

"Hey there," Lena said. "Is the tyke out for the night?"

"Totally. She worked hard on her playroom today." Vicki smiled. "And she loves it. Thanks, Lena. I can't quite tell how she organized it, but everything is where she wants it."

"I could get rid of that bed."

Vicki sat on the edge of the sofa. "I don't think you need to. It seems to have become the home for a bazillion stuffed animals."

"We should find some things to put on the walls," Lena remarked. "That old wallpaper just looks old, and the room hasn't been used in so long that if it ever had any charm, it was in another era."

Dan chuckled, and Vicki felt a smile lift her lips. "Krys seems happy with it."

"Krys put a lot of life into it," Lena agreed. "But I'm sure I could give her something cheerier to look at above little-girl height." She brightened. "Let's do that. Posters, whatever. Bright colors. I bet she'd love to help pick them."

Vicki had no doubt of that. "Just not too much," she said cautiously.

Lena eyed her inquisitively. "Why?"

Vicki hesitated, acutely aware that Dan would hear, and might take it wrong. "Well, our friends…" Yes, call them friends, not Hal's colleagues, not cops. "Every time they came to see us, they brought something for Krystal. That's why she has so many stuffed animals and toys. More than any child needs. Hal and I didn't want to spoil her, but…" Vicki shrugged, not knowing how to finish the thought.

"Well, thank goodness," Dan said.

Startled, she looked at him and found him almost grinning. "What?"

"Krystal was admiring the wolf on my T-shirt yesterday. You don't know how close I came to getting her a stuffed wolf. I guess that would have been the wrong thing to do."

Lena laughed. Vicki felt her cheeks warm. "It wouldn't have been wrong," she said swiftly. "I'm sure she would have loved it. It's just that she's spent most of past year living in a flood of gifts. That needs to slow down."

Dan winked. "Got it. I'll get the wolf next week."

In spite of everything, Vicki laughed. All of a sudden her heart felt a smidgeon lighter. "That'll work," she said.

Dan rose to get more coffee. Lena suggested he just bring the pot into the living room.

"So what's on the agenda for tomorrow?" Lena asked Vicki.

"Your house, your agenda."

Lena cocked an eyebrow at her. "You don't get off so easy. It's your house now, too. You still haven't gone through to tell me if I've labeled any furniture for removal that you might want to keep. And we need to get at your unpacking."

Vicki was glad Dan wasn't in the room at that moment, because what burst out of her sounded anything but adult. "Lena, this is so *hard.*"

Her aunt instantly came to sit beside her and hug her. "I know, my sweet girl. I know. Don't let me pressure you."

"It's not that," Vicki admitted. "It's that I seem to have made all the decisions I can make. I don't know if I can make any more. And I'm not even sure I made the right ones. What if this is all wrong for Krystal?"

Dan froze in the foyer as he heard what Vicki said. The worn oriental rug beneath his feet had silenced his steps, and he was certain neither of the women knew he was there. Should he go back into the kitchen? But the anguish in Vicki's voice riveted him to the spot.

He understood the torment of losing your spouse, and he was intimately acquainted with the decisions that eventually had to be made. Few of them were easy; all of them were painful. You could either turn your life into a living gravestone, or you could chose to move ahead.

But moving ahead meant making painful choices. The day he had realized that he needed to take his wife's clothing to the Red Cross had sent him over an emotional cliff edge. Lena talked about living in her family's museum. Well, he'd done that, too. He'd lived in a museum of his life with Callie. He supposed Vicki had done the same thing.

But his choices hadn't been as broad or sweeping as the ones Vicki had just made. She hadn't just closed up her own museum, but she'd left the only place familiar to her, everyone she knew, and she'd taken her daughter on the journey with her.

Hearing her fear that she might not have done right by Krystal pierced him. How she must have agonized over making the correct decisions.

He heard Lena speak again, quietly. "I'm sorry, my dear. I'm truly sorry. I keep wanting to be cheerful, and keep moving us along, and I forget how hard this must be. I've never had to do anything like it. It was different when your grandparents died. They were old, they were sick, it was time. And I didn't have to do anything except stay right here and let time do its work. You've chosen a much harder path."

"What if it's the wrong one?" Vicki asked, her voice strained.

"I can't guarantee it's not. Only time will tell. But I listened to you enough to know all the thought you put into deciding to move here. And I know that never at any point did you forget about your daughter."

Silence. Dan closed his eyes for a moment, absorbing Vicki's fears and pain. He didn't know what he could do about any of it, but he was determined to try. Then he heard Lena speak again.

"All right," she said, "no more decisions for you unless you feel like making them. There's really no rush, you know. I shouldn't have pressured you. Take a break. We'll sort out everything when you're ready."

Dan suddenly realized he'd been gone too long. After stepping backward on the rug to the kitchen door, he headed for the living room again, making his footsteps heavier this time.

When he entered the room, Lena was still sitting beside Vicki.

"Coffee, anyone?" he asked casually.

Chapter Three

Two days later, Vicki was beginning to feel that she had her feet under her again. She spent a couple hours unpacking her own belongings and arranging her bedroom, with Krystal's guidance, then suggested they take a walk to the park.

Krys, dressed like her mother in jeans and a T-shirt, liked the idea, but ran to her room to grab a teddy bear first.

Vicki wondered what to make of that. Krystal had never before seemed inclined to carry a stuffed animal with her. Maybe the girl was still feeling insecure. Vicki hid her concern behind a big smile, stopped to grab her purse and keys, then opened the front door.

A young woman stood there, hand raised to knock, and beside her was a girl of about Krys's age. The woman wore a summery halter dress, and the little girl was dressed in shorts and a sleeveless top with a pink bear on it. They looked almost like peas from the same pod with their shoulder-length auburn hair and hazel eyes.

"Hi," said Vicki. "Can I help you?"

The other woman smiled. "Well, we'd heard a new little girl had just moved in down the block. I'm Janine Dalrymple, and this is my daughter, Peggy. She's been badgering me to come meet you, but I figured you might need a day or two to settle in a bit."

Vicki immediately offered her hand. "Nice to meet you. I'm Vicki Templeton and this is my daughter, Krys." She glanced down at her, wondering how she would react. Vicki didn't have long to wait.

"Hi," Krys said to Peggy. "Mommy's taking me to the park. Do you know where it is?"

"The park is great," Peggy answered. "Slides 'n' swings and everything."

Before either woman could say another word, the girls were off together.

Janine regarded Vicki wryly. "I think we'd better keep up. How are you at the fifty-yard dash?"

Vicki laughed, quickly locked the door behind her and hurried along. She noticed the teddy bear had been left behind on the floor.

God, she hoped that was a good sign.

The next couple hours slid quickly by as the girls played and Janine filled Vicki in on enough local gossip that she wondered if she needed to keep a crib sheet.

"Oh, you'll hear it all again," Janine assured her. "And again. Eventually, you'll even remember the names. Little enough else to talk about around here except each other. Although… I wouldn't want you to worry…most talk is kind and general. We have to live together, and hard feelings could last a long time."

She looked toward the swings. "I see a couple of girls who are getting tired. Or at least Peggy is. Let's do this again."

"Absolutely."

Krystal practically skipped the whole way home, and after they left Janine and Peggy at their house, en route, she turned into a chatterbox, words tumbling over one another. It was the most animated Vicki had seen her daughter in ages.

Maybe, she thought, drawing in a deep breath of summer air as they walked beneath leafy trees, she hadn't been wrong to move. Maybe the shadows that had been haunting her had haunted Krys, as well.

Lena, who kept so-called banker's hours at her job, was already there, humming as she emptied some grocery bags. She looked up as Krys and Vicki joined her. "Don't you two look a sight for sore eyes. Good day?"

Krys didn't give her mother a chance to answer. She started babbling on about the park and Peggy, telling her great-aunt every delightful little moment, before running to the bathroom.

"Don't have to worry about conversation around that one." Lena grinned as she and Vicki finished putting groceries away.

"Not today, anyway."

"What did you think of Janine? At least I suppose it was Janine, seeing as how I just heard all about a little girl named Peggy."

Vicki laughed. "It was Janine. She spent the whole

time trying to clue me in on the town, and I'm not sure I remember a quarter of it."

"Most of it was probably old and outdated, anyway. We'll have new stuff to talk about next week."

Vicki laughed again. "So what can I do to help with dinner?"

"Not a dang thing. After all these years of cooking for one, and collaring Dan or the gals to come be extra mouths, I'm actually looking forward to making a meal big enough for four."

"Four?"

"I invited Dan over."

For some reason, this time Vicki didn't feel at all uncomfortable with the prospect. "Good. He's been scarce."

"All but invisible, if you ask me."

Vicki leaned back against the table, trying to stay out of Lena's way as she buzzed around. "You see him a lot?"

Lena glanced at her. "We're friends."

"I would have thought he'd have a more active social life."

"Than me? Thank you very much."

"I didn't mean it that way." Vicki felt her cheeks heat. The last thing she wanted to do was offend her aunt.

Lena turned from the groceries and eyed her. "I know you didn't. Like I said, we're friends. Just like I am with a bunch of gals. But if you're curious about him, ask him. The man's an open book."

Was she curious about him? Was that what had caused Vicki to speak in a way that had implied there might be something wrong with the man? Why should she care, anyway?

She couldn't answer those questions, but their existence scared her.

She didn't want to get involved. She didn't want another man in her life, most certainly not a cop. She shouldn't be curious about Dan at all...except that she was.

Oh, boy.

Dan had been trying to give Vicki the space she seemed to want, and life had cooperated. Last night there'd been a baseball game that he'd wound up umpiring, because their regular man had broken his foot. Tonight some of the deputies had suggested meeting at Mahoney's to watch a ball game on the big screen TV, and he'd considered it, but didn't really feel like it.

Lena's invitation had come as a relief, in a way. He could bow out of going to Mahoney's, and have a good excuse to see how Vicki was doing. Vicki and Krystal. He told himself he was more concerned about the little girl whose life had been upended, but he knew he was equally concerned about her mother. Been there, done that. He knew grief intimately, and he was worried about the woman.

When Callie had died, he'd stayed put for a few years, relying on his friends for distraction, and keeping as busy as he could. Occasionally, he had even allowed himself to wallow, not that his buddies would leave him alone for long.

Sometimes he'd resented their intrusions, but in retrospect he knew they'd helped him every single time they'd badgered him to come do something with them.

Vicki had chosen to kick that all to the curb. He knew everybody was different, but he still worried. Other than Lena, she didn't know a soul here.

He guessed that left him, for now, anyway. Except she had sort of made it clear that she didn't want him getting too involved. Maybe she was right. All that stuff about her being a cop's widow, deserving of support and whatever else she might need, was true. It was even good. Cops took care of each other and maybe she hadn't had time to discover it. But if someone else had been walking in her shoes, she and her late husband would have been among the people trying to help as they could.

But over the past couple days, Dan had become wary, and not just because she'd intimated she didn't want him to become too close to her and her daughter. He'd become wary of himself.

His first reaction on seeing her had been quickly swamped in the awareness of who she was, and concern for her, her daughter and Lena. But the mental image of when he'd first seen her come out the door had become engraved on his brain, and he couldn't dislodge it.

Vicki was sexy. Her tiny waist had been accentuated by the way she had knotted that shirt at her waist. Her hips flared perfectly, and when she bent over to lift something, he couldn't help noticing her rounded bottom. Eye candy.

The woman turned him on.

Not good. He didn't want another woman. Some part of him felt as if he'd be betraying Callie, even though it had been years, and that wasn't a feeling he could reason with. Then there was Vicki's clearly wounded state. And a little girl who might well resent any man who hung around her mother too much.

So while his response to her was all natural male, Dan couldn't afford to let it grow, not even a bit. All it could do was make a hash of everything, maybe even damage his friendship with Lena. He suspected *that* woman would react like a she-bear with cubs if she thought anyone might hurt her niece.

"Ah, hell," he said aloud as he showered after a long day of riding dusty roads and answering calls, most of which had turned out to be minor. He'd even had to pull a truck out of a ditch with his winch, all the while wondering if the driver, a ranch hand, had been drunk when it happened, but had had time to sober up and get rid of the evidence before Dan arrived. The guy had claimed to be waiting for a tow truck that hadn't yet shown.

It was possible, but not likely, so Dan had questioned him closely, hoping he put the fear of the law into him sufficiently that he wouldn't pop the top on a few beers again and then get behind the wheel. Or possibly enjoy the brewskis while he was driving.

It was easy out there on lonely county roads to sometimes get the idea you were all alone in the world. It was one of the reasons Dan liked patrolling, but it sometimes led people to do stupid things.

He glanced at the clock and realized it was time to get over to Lena's. The burst of activity rearranging the house had died down, or at least any part that might involve him. Lena had been all in a rush to get rid of furniture, enough of a rush that she'd labeled it all, but nothing on that front had happened since.

Of course, the other night he'd overheard Vicki saying she couldn't make any more decisions. He kind of understood that feeling, too. The way he had dithered about buying his own house…hell, it was a wonder the real estate agent hadn't thrown him out on his butt.

Now to go pretend he didn't feel attracted to Vicki, when in fact she was the first woman he'd felt attracted to since Callie… Didn't that beat all?

It also made him uneasy. Was he responding to Vicki especially, or was he just waking after a long period of quiescence? He didn't know. Dangerous ground, either way.

Krystal wanted to answer the door. Lena immediately said, "Let her. The worst thing that ever showed up on my doorstep was a guy selling life insurance."

So Vicki stayed in the kitchen with the delicious aromas of Lena's homemade mac and cheese—made with white cheddar and sausage instead of hot dogs— and tossed the salad.

She heard Krystal practically shriek, "Dan!" Then her daughter was off and running, relating everything she could about Peggy and the park. A short time later, Vicki heard footsteps approach and Dan's voice saying, "Howdy."

She turned and nearly gasped when she realized he'd picked Krystal up and was carrying her on his hip. "I want a horsey ride," Krys said. One of Hal's friends had taught her that, crawling around the floor on hands and knees while Krys straddled his back. Vicki's chest tightened a bit.

"Maybe we can get you a real horsey ride soon." Gently, Dan put the child down. "How are you ladies tonight?"

Their answers were drowned out by Krystal. "A real horsey? A big one?"

Dan squatted. "Maybe not so big for the first time, Krys. A deputy friend of mine, name of Sarah? Her husband has a horse ranch. He's got some ponies that might be great for your first ride. But only if it's okay with your mom."

That diverted Krystal straight over to Vicki, who, despite feeling a twinge of fear about what might happen to the girl if she fell from a horse, couldn't help laughing at her daughter's excitement. "We'll see," she said repeatedly. "We'll see. But don't bug me about it, kiddo."

Krys turned to Dan. "Bugging is bad."

"Yes, it is," he agreed, straightening. He looked at Vicki. "Did I put my foot in it?"

She shook her head with a smile. The offer had been intended kindly, and she wanted Krys to have every possible good experience. Vicki could endure the inevitable pestering.

"Go wash up for dinner," she told Krys. But her eyes seemed to have locked with Dan's, and she felt a warm tingle inside, accompanied by a slight speeding of her heart.

She turned swiftly back to the salad, resisting her response to the man. She'd cataloged his attractiveness at the very beginning, but it had been only that: noticing it but not responding to it. Now that she'd caught up some on her rest, her body seemed to be taking a different attitude.

She didn't want it. She absolutely did not want it. She wasn't ready for another man, any man, and least of all one who risked his life on a regular basis. One trip through that hell had been quite enough.

"Do I smell your famous mac and cheese?" Dan asked, returning everything to normal, especially for Vicki.

"That you do," Lena answered from the sink, where she was washing the cheese grater. "It's almost ready. Why don't you set the table?"

They gathered around the big round table in the kitchen instead of using the dining room. Krys was ravenous, and at first said very little. A couple times Vicki told her to slow down so she didn't get a tummy ache. Krys slowed down, but not for long. Her only comment was "I like white mac and cheese better than orange."

"A hit." Dan smiled. He was doing a pretty good job of eating his portion. "So, are you planning to go to the county fair this year?"

Lena shook her head slowly. "Hadn't thought about it. Krys should go, though. She'd probably like the rides. And, Vicki, I think you'd love the crafts. Some of the women around here make amazing quilts, and the knitting…well, if I could ever knit even stitches, I might go over to Cory's place and join one of her classes." Lena explained that there was a sewing and knitting shop just down the street from the diner. "You might like that, too."

"I might," Vicki agreed pleasantly, but her mind was back on the county fair. Had Lena just attempted some matchmaking, saying Krys and Vicki should go to the fair? The suggestion was hanging there as if she'd wanted Dan to say he'd take them.

But he didn't, and Vicki relaxed again.

"I'm not sure if I'll be working the fair or not,"

Dan said, after a bit more discussion from Lena. "The schedule is still up in the air, but since most of the deputies with kids want to take them, the rest of us will probably plug the holes."

Which, thought Vicki, was a good explanation for not offering to show them around, even if Lena had been trying to encourage it. Astonishment filled her as she realized she felt mildly disappointed. *Steady, girl.* No point in bargaining for trouble. "How long does it last?"

"It's a whole lot of setup for three days," Lena answered. "Friday afternoon through Sunday evening. The rodeo's on Saturday. And of course, one of those traveling carnivals always shows up."

"Why so short?"

"Most folks around here are awfully busy on their ranches," her aunt replied. "But summer is the time for fairs. What can I tell you? Imagine holding one when the weather turns cold."

"It's just a small fair," Dan explained. "We pretty much get overshadowed by the state fair, which offers a whole lot more for people who can get the time to go. Here it's…a community social, basically."

"Good description," Lena said approvingly. "Anyway, in one afternoon you can see everything you want to see, and fit in the rodeo, too. Now, I like our rodeo. It's mostly local cowboys who compete, not pros who are on the circuit, although we occasionally get one or two."

"That *would* be interesting. I've been to the one in Austin, but the rodeo is professional, and so is the entertainment."

Dan laughed. "You might hear a few local country musicians here."

"Don't forget the old guys with their fiddles," said Lena. "Always gets my foot tapping." She eyed Vicki. "A good place to meet people."

"Speaking of meeting people," Dan said, "I presume the Peggy that Krys was telling me about was Janine Dalrymple's little girl?"

"Yes, it was," Vicki replied. "They both came over this afternoon, and before I could even invite them in, the two girls were running down the street toward the park. We dashed to keep up. I like Janine."

"I thought you might," Dan said. "Salt of the earth."

"Did you ask her to come?" Vicki didn't know if she liked that. She preferred to think that Janine had come because she wanted to.

"Of course not," Dan said. "I passed her on the street and she asked about the rental truck, so I told her you were here."

So he wasn't trying to micromanage her life even in small ways. Vicki had been through enough of that. Something that had been coiled inside her let go, and she was able to enjoy the rest of the meal.

After they made short work of dishes, Krystal wanted to play a game. She asked Dan and he agreed. Soon they were all playing a very childish board game with Krys, whose brow knit with concentration. One of these days the girl would realize the whole game depended on luck, but right now she gave it the attention of a major tactician.

Finally, Lena claimed an aunt's prerogative. "Let me get Krys ready for bed and read her a story."

Krys jumped up. "Can I pick the story?"

"Of course you can." Lena looked at Vicki. "I don't know about you, but I could use some coffee."

"I'll make it."

"And I could use a walk," Dan said. "Been sitting too much today." He glanced at Vicki. "I can wait until you make the coffee if you want to take a turn around the block with me."

Summer evenings were long in Wyoming, and Vicki wondered when she had last taken a walk around a block. Part of her felt a little nervous, and part of her thought she was entirely too hypersensitive. A friend was going for a walk. It would have been rude of him not to ask her.

She wondered at herself. How had she gotten to the point of overreacting to friendly overtures? Why should she have been even a tiny bit disturbed if Dan had suggested to Janine that she bring her daughter over? It would have been a neighborly gesture.

For the first time Vicki considered the possibility that losing Hal had twisted her in some way. Suspicious of friendliness? Good heavens.

"I'd like that," she answered, then started making the coffee. "If you don't mind waiting."

"What, two minutes?" His tone evinced amusement. "Oh, man, I'm just panting to walk around the block. Vicki, I can't wait. Hurry! Hurry up!"

She had to laugh, and was still grinning when she finished preparing the coffee. "You're learning from Krys."

"That girl is a real experience. I never would have guessed a four-year-old could put an auctioneer to shame."

"She can spill those words out when she's excited."

Out on the street, with twilight beginning to settle, he said, "Vicki?"

"Yes?"

"If I was wrong to mention the horses, tell me. I don't suppose Krys is the type to forget."

"No, she's not." Vicki wished she'd brought a sweater. She'd left Austin at the height of summer, but the days were cooler here and the nights chilled fast.

"Well, I'm sorry if I caused you a headache."

"You didn't." She glanced sideways at him, and decided he had a great profile. He walked easily, like a man in great shape. "I never knew a girl who didn't want to ride a horse. If you hadn't mentioned it, someone else would have, and I really don't have an objection. I have to admit that I prefer the idea of a pony, though."

"Heck, no," he said humorously. "We'll put her on a stallion sixteen hands tall."

Another laugh escaped Vicki. "So your friend has ponies?"

"Yeah. Sarah Ironheart works with me. Her husband, Gideon, runs a stable, trains horses and gives trail rides. A decade or so ago he decided to get himself some American Shetlands. Kids often ride them."

"Sounds great to me. I think she'd like a horse closer to her size, at least to begin with. Then again," Vicki said wryly, "she might decide they terrify her. You never know with a child."

"I suppose you don't." He waved and called out a greeting to an older couple who were sitting in wooden rockers on their front porch.

"It's different here," she remarked suddenly.

"I suppose so. In what way do you mean?"

"Well, I was just noticing, this is a front porch town. Newer construction has banished the front porch to a backyard deck or patio."

He paused before answering. "You're right. I never really thought about it before."

"I never did, either. But it probably has a big impact on community dynamics. I wonder what started it."

He shook his head. They turned a corner and strolled on slowly. "I have no idea. TV? Lena tells me that when she was little sometimes neighbors would gather to watch TV together. These days, everyone has one at home."

"Well, I'm no social psychologist. It's just nice to walk down a street like this and see people out on their porches."

"The whole town isn't like this, though. After the Second World War some subdivisions were built. No front porches."

"Maybe it was a cost thing. I guess I should research it when I have some time."

He seemed comfortable with silence when it fell between them, so she didn't struggle to fill the void. She wondered if it had always been hard for her to chit-chat, or if this was a recent development. Honestly, she couldn't remember.

"Has Lena said any more about the furniture?" he asked.

"Not a peep." Vicki sighed. "That's my fault. I guess I need to get to it. I'm sorry."

"No need for you to be sorry. It's just that I need a heads-up to get some guys over to help. I may be strong, but that old furniture is heavy. Solid wood. Some of it I could trot around for her, but there are a few pieces where I'm going to be smart and say no way. They might as well be constructed of lead."

Vicki laughed quietly. "I've noticed. I tried to nudge an armoire around in my bedroom. No dice."

"I can help with it if you want. Just let me know."

She hesitated to speak. He was Lena's friend, after all, not yet hers. But still, she wanted to say something. "She kept telling me there was plenty of room, but I feel like we're crowding her out. And now she's saying she wanted to make the place over, anyway."

"She did. She mentioned it to me a few times before there was any possibility of you moving here. I've found that Lena can be as blunt as she needs to. If she had a problem with any of this, she'd say so."

Vicki looked at him, feeling an undeniable quiver of sexual attraction run through her. Was she trying to awaken as a woman again? Not good. "Thank you. So maybe I don't need to walk on eggshells?"

"Around Lena? No way." He flashed a smile. "She'd hate it if you did. That's one of the things I like about her. I can always count on her to tell me if I'm being a jerk."

A laugh bubbled out of Vicki. "You know, that's good to hear."

"I think she figured out a long time ago that leaving people to wonder what you were thinking created an awful lot of empty space for making trouble."

Vicki stopped walking. He halted beside her and faced her. "What?" he asked.

"I think that's a great observation. I'm going to keep that in mind." She smiled as they continued their walk, her heart feeling a little lighter.

From the outset she'd worried about Lena. It was

good to hear from someone else that her aunt didn't pull her punches. Now maybe Vicki could let go of that concern and just worry about the day-to-day matters.

As they rounded the last corner and were walking back to the house, she looked at Dan. "Are you as blunt as Lena?"

"Yes, when it matters. Your husband was a cop, so you should know. We learn to have difficult conversations."

His easy, comfortable reference to Hal reassured her in some odd way, as if setting her free to just be open about it all.

She hadn't wanted to even mention him, because she felt as if talking about him could depress everyone around her. Some of that had come in the other direction, too, as people tried to avoid reminding her of her losses.

That left a big void in her conversation, and in her heart. Hal had been her husband, a major part of her life, and grief was part of her life now. Avoiding it didn't change a thing.

"Thanks," she said as they reached the porch.

"For what?"

She looked up at him. "For mentioning Hal. I feel like I can't even talk about him. It makes people uneasy."

"I know what you mean. After Callie died there was a burst of remembrances from our friends, and then it was as if she was erased."

Vicki warmed to him. "Exactly. That's it exactly. Well, you go ahead and talk about Callie anytime you want, if I can do the same about Hal."

"Deal," Dan said.

At the door he stopped. "I need to get home. I've got to be in at five in the morning. Will you thank Lena for me again? It was a great dinner."

"I'll tell her."

Vicki waited, watching him cross the yard to his own front door. He was a good man, she decided. She could see why Lena liked him so much.

Inside she found her aunt curled up on her own sofa with a coffee and a book. "Nice walk?" she asked.

"Lovely. It's gorgeous out there this evening. Dan asked me to thank you again for a wonderful dinner. Was Krys okay?"

"Krys was a doll, and fell asleep long before Bartholomew Cubbins ditched his tenth hat."

Vicki giggled. "I wonder if she'll ever hear the end of that story."

"Someday she can read it to herself. I understand that children like repetition, but for those of us reading, not so much."

Vicki sat facing her aunt. "I'll look over the furniture tomorrow. But I want you to do it with me."

Lena waved a hand. "I already made my decisions. The only question is whether you disagree with any of them. And you still have some unpacking to do."

Vicki bit her lip. "Most of what's left is mementos of Hal. I'm not sure I want to unpack them, but I'm keeping them for Krystal. Can I put them in your attic or basement?"

"Not the basement. It gets damp sometimes. Set them aside and we'll get them into the attic."

A short while later, Vicki headed upstairs to shower and settle in for the night. The change to Mountain time might be part of it, or it could be due to all the hard work and stress over the past month, but she was going to bed earlier.

As she soaped herself in the shower, however, she experienced a strange moment when she felt lifted out of herself. Instead of her own hands running over her, her mind turned them into Dan's hands. Silky and smooth, gliding effortlessly over her every curve. Her breath started coming faster, and heat pooled between her thighs, a deliciously heavy and nearly forgotten sensation.

Then she snapped her eyes open. "No way," she said, her voice echoing in the shower. For the love of heaven, the man was a cop. If nothing else about him mattered, his being a police officer was a wall between them that she didn't even want to think about climbing.

She'd had enough of that. More than enough.

Angry with herself, she turned down the temperature of the water until it felt slightly cold.

If she ever, *ever* again had a love relationship, it wasn't going to be with a man who, every time he walked out the door, left her wondering if he'd come back alive. It had been hard enough when part of her believed that couldn't happen to Hal.

But then it had. And it hadn't even happened when he was on duty. No, he'd made a simple run to the convenience store because they were out of milk. A robbery. A man with a gun, and valiant Hal stepping into it like the cop he was. The robber was in jail, but Hal was in the ground.

No, she wasn't ever going to risk that again. And she wasn't going to risk putting her daughter through it. No way.

Stepping out of the shower, Vicki scrubbed her body

with a towel until it felt as if she'd removed an entire layer of skin. She glanced in the mirror and saw a woman filled with furious determination.

Her hair, as it began to dry, started to curl wildly. Ruthlessly, she brushed it straight and caught it in a ponytail. Hal had liked those curls. She had no desire to flaunt them ever again.

Chapter Four

A week later, on Saturday, Dan showed up with four other guys to help move the furniture Lena had decided to get rid of. Vicki and Krys were banished to the park, while Lena remained to supervise.

Krys wanted to know why Aunt Lena was moving out.

"She's not moving out, sweetie. She's making room."

"For us? She's nice."

"I like her. I guess you do, too?"

"Yeah." Krystal grinned up at Vicki. "I like it here."

"Really?" Her heart skipped a few beats as an extraordinary sense of relief flooded her. She'd feared her decision to move primarily because of Krystal, but apparently everything was going to be all right.

"Yup," said Krystal, who had recently picked up the

affirmative from Peggy. "I like Peggy and her mommy, too. And Dan."

"Of course." Dan especially, since he'd been remarkably patient with the girl, playing board games and Old Maid with her when he had the time. Often he did not, because, Vicki had learned, he coached a recreational soccer team for girls, and played on a baseball team that consisted primarily of local deputies. They often faced off against another local team.

Just last evening, he had taken Krys outside with a soccer ball and started teaching her how to kick it. Vicki had been surprised at how reluctant Krys was to kick the ball.

"That's not unusual," Dan told her. "This is the first hump we have to get over with almost all the kids. Later we worry about the other stuff." He turned. "No, not with the toes, Krys. Remember."

The girl's scowl of concentration had remained with Vicki. It had been adorable.

Now at the park, awaiting the arrival of Janine and Peggy, Krys asked, "When can I ride a horsey?"

Vicki looked at her.

"I'm a bug?" Krys asked.

Vicki pressed her lips together so she wouldn't laugh. "Uh, no, you're not a bug. But I can't answer that question, so you shouldn't bug me about it."

"Who can tell me?" Krys demanded.

"We can't do it until Dan can make the arrangements."

Krys's brow furrowed. "Like what?"

"Like, he's got to have the time off, and then he has to talk to his friend who has the horses, and his friend has to have the time to give you a ride."

"Sheesh. I'll never ride a horsey."

"Of course you will. Dan will see to it." Of that she had not the least doubt, after the past week or so. The man's middle name should be Reliable.

Janine and Peggy couldn't stay for long because Janine had to go clean her ill mother's house and make dinner for her. Vicki almost offered to keep Peggy for the rest of the day, then realized she couldn't. Until Lena's house was sorted out, they had to stay out of the way.

Some other children arrived to play, but they were all much older and didn't show any interest in Krys, understandably enough, so soon the child was left to her own devices. And soon she was growing bored.

"Let's go for a walk downtown," Vicki suggested, not knowing what else to do. If they went back to the house, she might enjoy watching sweating men grunting as they moved furniture, but Krys would continue to be bored and would probably manage to get underfoot. Vicki also suspected Krys's presence would put a damper on the males' most enjoyable pastime: cussing inventively while they worked.

She almost laughed at her own train of thought. By the time they walked the few blocks, Krys was beginning to drag her feet. Glancing at her watch, Vicki realized it was nearly lunchtime. Instead of wandering through stores, she took her daughter to the diner, hoping food would perk her up.

Vicki checked her cell phone for messages, but had none, which meant they weren't through with clearing the house. When she thought about the big pieces of furniture Lena wanted moved, she wondered if the job would even be done today.

The diner wasn't too busy yet, so they were able to get a small booth near the front window. Krys had no doubt about what she wanted: a hamburger. It arrived with the usual mountain of fries. Vicki didn't feel very hungry, so she ordered a chef's salad. It looked big enough to feed a crowd.

"Why's that lady so grumpy?" Krys asked, after Maude slammed their plates down.

"She's not grumpy," said a familiar voice. "She's Maude."

"Dan!" Krystal shrieked and wormed her way out of the booth to reach up for a hug. Dan obliged her, then set her on her bench and slid in beside her.

"Hi," he said to Vicki. "Tyke's getting tired?"

"A little. I think food will rev her up. Is the job done?"

"Not quite. We're taking a lunch break. I told Lena I'd bring back something for her. She wanted to feed us, but that's just a little bit difficult right now." He was smiling and relaxed, and he looked down at Krys. "Are you getting tired of not being able to go home?"

"Which home?" Krys asked.

Dan looked nonplussed. Vicki felt her heart stutter. "This is our home now," she said quietly.

"I know." Krys picked up another fry and bit into it. In her small hand it looked gigantic.

Vicki looked at Dan and saw understanding in his gaze. She guessed her concern had been written all over her face.

"What about my horsey ride?" Krystal asked.

"Honey…" Vicki instinctively wanted to hush her. It was important to learn not to press people for gifts. But Dan forestalled her.

"Next weekend," he said. "Gideon's going to bring his ponies to the fair, and he promised me you could ride as long as you want."

Krystal brightened as if a lightbulb had turned on inside her. "Next week? How many days?" She looked at her hands. "Seven. Seven days. That's a long time." But she didn't stop smiling.

"Thank you," Vicki said to Dan.

He smiled. "Plenty of other stuff planned, too. Listen, if you want to bring Krystal home, I think you can now. We moved everything from upstairs down, so she can use her playroom, bedroom and bathroom, and there won't be anything dangerous on the stairs."

Vicki blinked. "My, you have been busy."

"Many hands and all that." He started to ease out of the booth. "I think that's my carryout. Want me to get Maude to wrap yours up? I've got the car and I can drive you home."

Vicki looked at her daughter, who, despite that burst of excitement over the idea of the horse ride, was now fiddling with her food more than eating it. Vicki began to wonder if this was just fatigue or something else. "Thanks. I think we'd both like that."

"I don't have a booster seat for her. I should probably ticket myself."

A laugh escaped Vicki. "I didn't think of that. I'm so used to having one in my car. Okay, I'll walk her home. Krys, are you done eating?"

She nodded. "Doesn't taste good."

Vicki immediately went on high alert. She reached across the table and tried a fry. "They're fine. Okay, sweetie, we're going to put your lunch in a box and get you home."

"You think she's getting sick?" Dan asked.

"I don't know. Maybe."

"Let me take care of your lunches. You head on home with her right now. Or I could go get your car, or the booster seat from it."

It seemed as if every minute Vicki spent with this man, she warmed to him more. Alarm bells clanged, but they were muffled by her concern for Krystal. Besides, liking a man was a long way from being involved.

"God, am I stupid," he said suddenly.

Startled, she gaped at him. "What?"

"Stay here. Give me five. Maude," he called out, "I'll be right back for those lunches. Could you pack these up, please? And just add them to my tab."

He dashed out the door. Maude clomped over to the table with two boxes for the meals. "You want me to fill them?"

"I can do that, thank you." Then Vicki saw the woman's face soften, just a teeny bit.

"The little one don't look so good. I'll get you a bag."

Vicki just finished moving the food into the foam containers when she saw Dan return out front, carrying a booster seat. Where had that come from?

It took him only a minute to install it in the back of his SUV, and then he came back into the diner. "All set," he said cheerfully.

He stopped at the register to pay the bill, and Vicki clearly heard Maude say, "On the house. You just take care of that little girl."

It seemed there was a heart of gold hidden beneath that rough, irritable exterior.

"Where did the seat come from?" Vicki asked as she adjusted the straps for Krys.

"The sheriff's office has about a dozen of them. I don't know how I could have spaced it."

"Why so many?"

"Community effort to ensure no kid rides unprotected just because their parents can't afford a seat. When they're no longer needed, they come back to us, we get 'em cleaned and checked out, and if they're still usable, they get used again."

"What a great idea!"

"I bet your husband's department did the same thing. We're not exactly unique that way. I went to a conference once and a cop from Georgia explained it to me like this. He said once you see what can happen to a kid who isn't properly secured, you never want to see it again. Thank God, I've never seen it."

Vicki looked at him. "Hal did once. He had to take time off and he spent three days cussing nonstop."

Dan touched her shoulder. "Did he get some professional help?"

"Of course not," she said with a bitterness that surprised her. "Cops don't want that on their records."

Dan didn't say another word. He loaded the bags into the back, then held the passenger door open for her.

Whatever he thought about professional help and cops who didn't get it, he never said.

That had been the other downside to being a cop's wife, Vicki thought as she rocked beside Krystal's bed. The girl hadn't argued about taking a nap, a sure sign that she wasn't feeling well. Sounds from downstairs were muted, as if the men helping to move Lena's furniture were trying to be quiet.

Which gave Vicki perhaps too much time to think. Being a cop's wife had been difficult in more than one way. Vicki sometimes wondered how so many women handled it. By not thinking about it? By staying busy? Staying busy had been her choice, a way to avoid worrying every time he went out the door. Maybe if they'd been married longer she might have become inured to it. At least until the violence struck too close to home. She'd seen the other wives after Hal died, had noticed how they'd clung a little closer to their men. Every so often, the awful possibilities just couldn't be ignored.

But there'd been the other stuff, too. Hal had tried not to bring it home, but even in the five years of their dating and marriage, she'd begun to see changes in him. While he wouldn't talk about the ugly matters, she was sure there were plenty of them, judging by his occasional angry outbursts, and by the nights she awoke to find him out of bed and pacing.

Surprisingly, it had been a newspaper reporter who had told her, "We all get some PTSD. Cops, firemen, EMTs, reporters. You can't avoid it, because every so often you're going to deal with something so terrible you can't close your eyes without seeing it."

Since Hal wouldn't talk to her about things that disturbed him, probably because he was trying to protect her, she finally had learned to just let him be. After a few days, he wouldn't be so angry or irritable, and he wouldn't spend hours outside by himself shooting hoops at a nearby park. Somehow he always found his way back, and it wasn't as if it happened constantly.

But at some level she'd been aware of what he might

be dealing with, and considered herself lucky that she never had to go to the scene of an accident or shooting. She was touched, too, by the way he sheltered her.

Hal was a good man, she thought, as she watched her daughter sleep. Like so many cops, he'd joined the force to help and protect people. Of course, Vicki had met the other kind, the thrill seekers, the tough guys, but Hal hadn't invited them into his personal circle.

Reaching out, she touched Krys's forehead and thought it felt just a tiny bit warm. Vicki was sure she'd packed a thermometer, but couldn't remember unpacking it. Well, it would be easy enough to get another, she supposed, if Krys started to feel too hot.

Lena poked her head in, asking in a whisper, "How's she doing?"

"Out like a light. Maybe a bit warm. I'm not sure because she's sleeping." Like her father, Krystal seemed to radiate heat when she slept.

"Need a thermometer? Want to go to the doctor?"

This was ridiculous, Vicki thought, the two of them whispering across the large room. She eased out of the rocker and tiptoed over to the door so she could step into the hallway. She was surprised to see Dan near the top of the stairs.

"How is she?" he asked.

All thoughts about the dangers of caring about a cop flew from her head as his concern touched her. She was making too much of nothing. Dan was just a nice man, and he truly seemed to like Krystal. Her daughter needed that. "I think she's okay. If she's sick, it's not bad."

"I can call my doctor to see her, if you get worried at

any point," Lena offered. "Or there's the minor emergency clinic the hospital started a couple of years ago."

"I don't think we've reached that level."

"We're almost done downstairs," Dan said. "And by the way, I noticed you never ate lunch. Want me to bring your salad up?"

Vicki felt wrapped in caring. She'd been wrapped in it before and had struggled to break free, but somehow this felt different. "Thanks, both of you. I'm not hungry right now."

Lena patted her arm. "Of course not. When we're done below, we'll let you know. Maybe we can bring Krys downstairs if you want to keep an eye on her."

It was different here, Vicki thought, as she returned to the bedroom and sat again in the rocker. At home—her former home—she had been able to keep an eye on Krystal from the next room. No stairs between, no big gaping spaces as at Lena's house. Taking Krys downstairs and setting her up on the couch might be a good idea.

Assuming she didn't feel better when she woke.

Maybe it was just all the accumulated stress of the move and the changes. Maybe she was just tuckered out. Vicki could sure identify with that. Nothing was familiar any longer. The old routines were all broken. It was a bit tiring and stressful even for her. How much more so for Krystal?

Sitting and rocking, forced into a quiet moment by life, Vicki thought over the past year, even the painful times, and once again sorted her priorities.

She knew she needed to move on. She didn't need Hal to tell her; it's what he would have wanted. The question was, how much did she want it?

Evidently, enough to move here, away from everything and everyone that reminded her of Hal. Except for her daughter, of course. Looking at Krys would forever remind her that Hal had lived, loved and laughed with her. That he'd been the center of her existence for a long time.

Some things couldn't be left behind. No way.

Nor should they be.

Krys woke a couple hours later. She was hungry and thirsty, and a little cranky. Vicki pressed her palm to her daughter's forehead, didn't think she felt feverish, and after a trip to the bathroom, they headed downstairs.

The house suddenly looked empty.

"What happened, Mommy?" Krys asked when they were halfway down the steps.

"I guess Aunt Lena got rid of everything she didn't want."

"This is a big house!"

Indeed it was. It had pretty much absorbed two extra people and their belongings, while appearing only slightly crowded once the majority of boxes had disappeared. Now it looked almost empty.

Lena was in the kitchen cooking dinner, and turned at once to ask Krys how she was.

"Hungry," she answered promptly.

"I think I can do something about that," Lena replied.

"I can just get her lunch out."

Lena shook her head. "I can do better than a hamburger." She looked at Krys. "Watermelon?"

Krys clapped her hands together. "I love watermelon!"

"I thought you might." Still smiling, Lena looked at Vicki. "Dinner won't be for a while. I'm roasting a fat old chicken. Dan will be back. He said he'd move the boxes you want stored up in the attic."

"Wow. He's already done a lot today."

Lena nodded. "I know. But these guys…you'd think they just wanted to get all this done, the sooner the better." She winked, making Vicki laugh, and went to the refrigerator to pull out a watermelon that had already been sliced into wedges.

Krystal tucked into the watermelon, not caring that she smeared her face and got covered with juice. Vicki watched her, smiling faintly, wondering at what point in life people started to shed the exuberance of childhood. What did it matter if her daughter got covered with watermelon juice? It could all be washed up.

So of course, watching all this, she ate her own slices carefully. She could have laughed at her own absurdity. "What can I do to help?" she asked Lena.

"Just keep me company. I'm in a cooking mood. Days will come when I'll holler for you to take over the chore for me, but right now it doesn't feel like one."

"I should thank everyone who came to help with all of this."

"I already did. But one of these days, if you want, we can have them and their families over for a barbecue out back."

Vicki almost agreed, but the words stalled in her throat. It would be just like it had been before, only the faces and names would change.

She spoke to Krys instead. "Are you feeling better?"

Her daughter nodded, her mouth full of watermelon.

So maybe it had been fatigue brought on by all the stimulation. Krys's entire world had changed, and now everything was new. But Vicki had already thought of that. She guessed the question she really wanted to ask, and didn't know if her daughter could even begin to answer, was whether she was homesick.

Vicki herself was past homesickness. Her entire heart centered around Krystal now, and she didn't even miss the home she had shared with Hal. She didn't miss any of it—not the town, lovely though it was, not the shady streets and lanes in some of the older areas, not the beauty of the Hill Country to the west, nor even her friends.

It was as if she had sliced something off at some point.

Or she could just be fooling herself.

Later that evening, Lena took Krystal up to bed again. It had become a new routine, every other night Lena tucking Krys in and reading to her.

Tonight, as they headed upstairs, Lena looked back at Vicki, and at Dan, who had once again joined them for dinner. "Why don't you two take a walk or something? Get out of here for a while. Sometimes a woman needs to be something besides a mother."

Startled, Vicki looked at Dan, who just shrugged, as if he didn't get it, either. But there was a warm light in his eyes, and his gaze seemed to pass over her appreciatively. She was startled again by the strong tug of attraction she felt toward him, but this time didn't evade it. She trusted him now not to get out of line, and it did her ego some good to know the attraction wasn't one-sided. She also liked him far better in jeans and a fleece shirt than in his uniform.

Outside on the street, this time with a royal-blue hoodie to ward of the evening chill, Vicki asked, "What did she mean by that?"

"You'll have to ask her," Dan answered. "I'm just following orders."

Vicki might have taken umbrage, except that he sounded so amused. She had to laugh. "Is that what we're doing?"

"So it appears. A woman tells me to get out of her house and take a hike, I go."

Vicki laughed even harder. "It almost sounded like that."

"Maybe Lena needs some quiet after today. We sure made enough of a ruckus."

"But you were helping us out."

"Doesn't mean the helpers don't wear out the helpee."

"True." A shadow seemed to pass through Vicki, saddening her somehow and leaving her feeling a little cold inside. "Dan?"

"Yeah?"

"Do you know why I moved here?"

"Are you asking me or do you want to tell me?"

She hesitated. "I don't want to offend you. And I wondered how much Lena told you. Heck, I'm not even sure how much I told Lena."

"All she told me was that she'd been asking you to come, and that you started to feel a need to move on. Beyond that, I'm in the dark."

"Okay."

They walked in silence. He didn't press her, and Vicki was grateful for that. But he also didn't give her

the feeling that he didn't care. She could feel his attention as surely as if he wore a sign, but he wasn't going
to push her. Hal would have pushed her. Hal had hated
it when he'd sensed she was thinking about something
but wasn't sharing it. For the first time she realized how
much that had annoyed her.

"Sometimes," she said, "I just need to think things
through on my own."

"Understandable." They had reached the park. "Do
you want to warm a bench for a while, or keep walking?"

"The walking feels good." So they kept on. Twilight
was beginning to fade into night, and a gentle breeze
whispered in the trees.

"Hal always wanted to know what I thinking," she
said. "And sometimes I just wasn't ready to talk about
it. I wasn't sure what I was feeling, wasn't sure where
it was going, it was just something working around
in my head, you know? A lot of the time it was about
some child in one of my classes, but sometimes it was
about other things. Regardless, I get quiet when I'm
working something through."

"And he didn't like that."

"Not at all."

"Well, it's not my place to offer an opinion on that."

"Oh, go ahead."

Dan laughed quietly. "I've found it's best to keep my
thoughts to myself until I understand them."

She halted sharply and looked at him. Overhead, a
streetlight winked on, making him look strange, yet
still familiar. "Exactly!"

His smile widened. "A meeting of minds?"

"Oh, yeah. Hal wasn't like that. Well, not exactly.

When something from work really troubled him, he could turn into a clam. I'd know it only from the way he acted, and if I got any details it was from the newspaper. He was trying to protect me, I guess. But he could clam up."

"And you never could?"

"He didn't like it."

"So feel free to be a clam with me. I can take it."

She bet he could. She wrapped her arms around herself. "So I'm going to tell you something, and I don't want you to think it's in any way about you, because it's not."

He paused before responding. "Maybe we should have taken one of those benches." His tone conveyed humor.

"Oh, cut it out," she said, a tremor of laughter in her voice. "It's not about you. It's about a cop thing."

"Well, I'm a cop."

"Not in the way I'm going to talk about."

"Have at it, then."

But still she hesitated. When she thought about the subject, it felt one way, but she suspected she was going to sound like an ungrateful witch when she said it out loud. Steeling herself, she took the leap.

"I left Austin because I was feeling smothered."

He waited, letting her find her own way through. They approached the downtown area, but he waved his hand and they turned along another residential street. A Conard City police car started rolling slowly by, then came to a halt beside them. "Hey, Dan," said a voice from inside.

"How's it going, Jake?" Dan asked, pausing to face the car.

"Boring. As usual. Even the kids are behaving to-night."

"Vicki Templeton, this is Jake Madison, our chief of police."

"Nice to meet you."

"I'd heard you moved to town," the chief said. "I'd have helped except I'm holding down two jobs."

"Jake ranches, too," Dan explained.

"That's a lot to do," Vicki remarked.

"Keeps me out of trouble. You two enjoy your walk. Vicki, I'll tell my wife, Nora, to give you a call some-time. Or you can stop in the library and meet her. She works there three days a week. See you around."

Then the vehicle continued down the street.

Vicki didn't move for a minute. "Was that a cop thing?" she asked finally.

"What? Suggesting you meet his wife?"

"Yeah."

"I don't know. I doubt it. Why?"

God, this was going to sound awful. Maybe she shouldn't even bring it up. But then Dan astonished her. Reaching out, he gripped her hand gently and tugged until she started walking with him again. The warmth of his touch triggered an instant heat deep within her, and for a few moments she wanted to pull herself out of her thoughts and take a different direction.

Avoid the whole thing.

"You wanna tell me about it?"

Then it struck her that she needed to test her reaction against someone like Dan. Someone who could under-stand and maybe explain, and maybe tell her whether it would be the same here, or if that friendly little conver-sation had been just that, a friendly little conversation.

"I felt smothered back home." She repeated the claim, this time more vehemently.

"By what?"

"By Hal's colleagues and their families. Oh, God, I sound awful. It's just that… I never had a weekend to myself. My teacher friends gave me more space, but Hal's friends…it was like they were afraid that if I had to deal with a weekend alone, I might do something drastic."

Dan tightened his hold on her hand. "That's how they made you feel?"

"Yes."

"Oh, man. Maybe they went a little overboard."

"More than a little. I understand the point of the blue wall, and I was grateful, especially at first. But then it was as if I had to keep dancing or I'd have one of the women on my doorstep, wondering if I was all right. Oh, this is so hard to explain. But eventually, I got to thinking that I'd never be able to move on if I didn't move away. I was surrounded by so much caring I felt like I couldn't breathe. And it sounds just awful to say it."

She waited for his reaction, and glanced at him repeatedly, trying to read some reaction on his face. But as she had noted before, Dan's face revealed very little unless he chose to let it. Right now it was a mask, not stony, just unrevealing.

"After Callie died," he said, "I got the same sort of treatment. I appreciated it. Sometimes I wonder what I would have done during those last few months of her life if I hadn't had that support. It was different for me because we knew Callie was dying. And maybe because I'm a guy and people felt they couldn't push too hard. I don't know. The thing that irritated me most was that afterward, nobody seemed to want to talk about her. But we mentioned that last time we took a walk. I needed to talk about her, Vicki."

"Of course you did. I needed to talk about Hal. I still do sometimes."

"So, I kind of get it. I felt silenced. You felt smothered. And all of it with the best intentions in the world."

She nodded. "Exactly. The best intentions. Which makes it hard to say to somebody 'I don't want to come to your barbecue this weekend because I really need some time alone.'"

"Yeah."

Dan turned at another corner, and Vicki realized they were wandering even farther from Lena's. Good, because she wasn't ready to head back. She needed this break, and oddly, Dan's presence was giving her something, letting her lance an old emotional sore.

"Maybe I'm being unfair," she said after a bit.

"I don't think fairness applies to how we feel."

"No, of course it doesn't. But they are all good people, Dan. It's just that I started to feel as if I was always going to be Hal's widow. The person everyone felt an obligation to look after, but…oh, I don't know. Of course I'm Hal's widow. But I'm other things, too, and those other things were vanishing under the weight of being Hal's widow. I can't explain it any better than that."

"Frozen in time," he remarked.

"Or frozen in a role." She had certainly begun to feel that she'd have no other future, the way things were going. And she was equally positive no one had meant to make her feel that way. "I guess I should have just told them, instead of running away. Stood up to it. At the very least I wouldn't have put Krystal through all this."

"Krystal's going to be fine. At her age, you're the major stability in her life. If she were older, it might be different."

Vicki thought about that and decided at least to some extent he was right. Even at Krys's preschool the kids had been changing constantly. She hadn't had one friend who'd remained for an entire year. Young families moving up tended to move a lot. Or look for a more convenient day care, or whatever. Among Hal's friends and Vicki's teacher friends, there had been no other girls Krystal's age. Odd, but there it was.

So maybe here in this town, where change came slowly, Krys could find that kind of stability, as well. Certainly she and Peggy had become best buds. Whether that would last, who knew, but the start had been made.

Then there was Vicki herself. This was an odd kind of place to come make a new life, but she loved Lena, and the chance to move in with her had proved impossible to resist. She'd applied for her state teaching license and was sure she could find a job eventually, at some level, as a teacher around here. In the meantime she had plenty to do getting herself and Krys settled into life here.

Then, of course, there was Dan, who was still holding her hand as if it were the most ordinary thing in the world. Once again she noticed the warmth of his palm clasped to hers, the strength of the fingers tangled with hers. Damn, something about him called to her, but it could never be, simply because he was a cop.

"I'm not making you feel smothered, am I?"

Startled, she looked at him. "No. How could you think that? You've been helpful, but you haven't been hovering."

He laughed quietly. "Good. When you first arrived I had two thoughts. You were Lena's niece and I'm crazy about Lena, so I wanted to make you feel at home. The second was…wait for it…"

"Duty," she answered. "Caring for the cop's widow and kid." She didn't know whether to laugh or cry. It was everywhere.

"Of course," he answered easily. "Nothing wrong with it. Even around here where the job is rarely dangerous, we all like knowing that we can depend on the others to keep an eye on our families. Nothing wrong with that. But I can see how it might go too far. And everyone's different, with different needs."

She sidestepped a little to avoid a place where the sidewalk was cracked and had heaved up. His hand seemed to steady her.

"Promise me something," he said.

"If I can."

"If I start to smother you, you'll tell me. I wouldn't want to do that."

"I'm not sure you could," she answered honestly. "But I promise."

He seemed to hesitate, very unlike him. "There was a third reason I wanted to help out," he said slowly.

"What was that?"

He surprised her. He stopped walking, and when she turned to face him, he took her gently by the shoulders. Before she understood what he was doing, he leaned in and kissed her lightly on the lips. Just a gentle kiss, the

merest touching of their mouths, but she felt an electric
shock run through her, felt something long quiescent
spring to heated life.

Instantly, fear slammed her. *No. Not with him. Not
with a cop.*

But he let go of her before she could react, and resumed their walk. "Reason number three. You're a
wonderfully attractive woman. But don't worry about
it. That was just an experiment."

An experiment? God, now she felt utterly confused.
The warring emotions inside her were bad enough, but
now she had to wonder how his experiment had turned
out. Good? Bad? Indifferent?

Surprisingly, she hoped she hadn't left him cold.

"Dan?"

He paused again, touched her lips lightly with his
fingertip. "You don't need to say anything. Like I said,
you're an attractive woman. Nice kiss. But you're not
ready, are you."

He could tell all that? What, had she been sending
out smoke signals? She couldn't even remember if she'd
reacted to his kiss in any way other than to experience
an astonishing flood of sexual longing, something that
had been buried for a long time now. Then she remembered she had stiffened. Embarrassment flooded her,
but she couldn't say anything.

"So tell me more about Hal," Dan said.

All of a sudden, she didn't want to talk about Hal.
She wanted to talk about herself, about all the difficulties, about her fears, about her unexpected new
yearnings. Or maybe not talk, but certainly think it
all through again.

Maybe that was part of her problem, though. Initially paralyzed by shock and grief, she had drifted like a leaf on the breeze. But as she'd come out of shock, she'd turned to activity, to busyness, to focusing on everything outside herself. Then she had become concerned that no matter how busy she got, nothing was changing. She was taking no step in any direction to start a new life. Not one.

For a while, concern about Krystal had been her excuse, but finally Vicki had realized that the way she was existing couldn't possibly be good for her daughter. Not one new or interesting thing had entered their lives. They had settled into a routine within the comforting walls provided by Hal's friends. That was when she had realized that she was beginning to feel constricted. Smothered.

She blamed Hal's friends, but the truth was she had let them build that cocoon around her. Invited it. She could have stopped them at any time, could have created her own space, sought out her own friends.

But no, it had been easy just to drift. The easiest way to deal. Until finally the only solution she could see was to uproot herself and her daughter?

"Vicki?"

They were getting closer to home now, and part of her wanted to run away, just run away and hide in a cave. But she'd been doing that for more than a year now, until some survival instinct had brought her here.

"Vicki, are you okay?"

Of course he was wondering. He'd kissed her, she'd become outwardly stiff despite the inner firestorm of response, then he'd asked her about Hal and she hadn't answered. Dan must be wondering if she was furious with him.

"I'm mad at myself."

"Whatever for?" he asked.

"Because I just realized... Hal's friends weren't smothering me. I let them. I wanted them to. I was hiding in them."

Dan walked a bit before responding. She had noticed how unwilling he seemed to be to comment on her. She wondered if that was because he figured she was entitled to her own thoughts and reactions, or if it was because he just didn't know what to say.

Funny, she'd never thought of herself as some kind of puzzle box.

"I don't see anything wrong with that," he said finally. They could see the front porch of Lena's house now. Lights glowed from within as the summer night slowly deepened. "Healing is a very individual process. I don't think it's wrong to lean on others for whatever we need at the time, not if they're willing."

"Maybe not, but I think I took it to an extreme. And then when I realized I needed to make some changes, I practically threw it all in their faces by leaving town."

"I would bet they didn't take it that way. They were probably glad to see you ready to move on."

"Relieved, probably."

"Dang, Vicki."

"What? I must have been a drag."

"Just tell me one thing. Have you heard from any of them since you left?"

She thought immediately of all the texts she had been receiving. "I get text messages. Several a day."

"If they really wanted to be shed of you, they wouldn't be doing that."

He was right. She shook her head at herself, and

wondered what other parts of her had vanished with Hal. His death had changed her inalterably. Maybe it was time to take a measure of the ways.

"Darn it," she said.

"What?"

"Just everything. I've screwed it all up and now I have to figure out how to fix it."

"Fix what?" They stopped in front of Lena's house, alone on a quiet street, the porch only six paces away.

"I took a huge leap into the unknown out of a manufactured sense of desperation, and I took my daughter with me. I may have been reacting more than reasoning."

"I don't know," he answered.

She gave him points for honesty. No calm, soothing words or aphorisms.

He looked away for a few beats, then spoke slowly. "It was awful when Callie got sick. Maybe when she finally died I felt some relief. For her. For me. Selfish, maybe, or just realistic. Those last few months were so hard on her. Then it hit me that I'd never see her again. I don't have to tell you what that felt like. Purely selfish then."

"Really?"

"Unlike you, I'd watched my wife waste away and suffer tremendous pain. I can't help but think my grief was selfish, because she'd had enough, and wanting to keep her longer…well, that wasn't for her benefit, was it?"

"Dan…" Vicki reached out to touch his arm, feeling such an ache for him. It reached past all her defenses, spearing her.

"It's all right." He gave her a crooked smile. "Long

time ago, and I've worked through it. Grief is really something, though. It's not enough that we miss someone so much we can barely stand it, but it gets all mixed up with other stuff, like guilt. Kinda like walking across a glacier, never knowing when you'll hit the next crevasse."

She nodded, agreeing with him. She let her hand fall from his arm.

"And as for that stages-of-grief thing... I don't know about you, but they come in no particular order, and some of them keep popping up again for another go-round. It does start to get easier, though, Vicki. I can promise you that much." He looked toward the house. "Say good-night to Lena for me. I'll check with her tomorrow."

Vicki watched him turn and walk across to his own front door. He waved once, then disappeared inside.

For the first time she saw Dan Casey as a man who could understand her.

Chapter Five

"When can we leave?" Krystal demanded, practically bouncing with impatience. "Soon?"

"Soon," Vicki answered. The day of the county fair had arrived. For the past week, she and Lena had spent a lot of time putting prices on the things Lena intended to sell out of her garage that day. Vicki had often thought the prices too low.

"I just want it gone," Lena had answered.

"You can always haggle. Start higher."

"Ah, the garage sale guru."

Vicki had laughed. "People expect to bargain. They're not going to pay your asking price, no matter how low."

Muttering something about interfering nieces, Lena had complied. She'd been running an ad in the local paper all week, and Vicki and Krystal had busied themselves putting up signs on light poles and passing out fliers. If anyone in town hadn't heard of the sale, it would be a miracle.

Vicki gathered a handful of fliers to take with her to the fair, and glanced at her daughter. "Ready?"

Krys looked about ready to pop. "Yeah," she said eagerly. "My pony ride. And cotton candy."

"There's other stuff, too," Vicki reminded her, but these two things had been Krys's major preoccupation all week.

They took the car, because Vicki fully expected that by the time Krys wanted to leave, she was going to be awfully tired. Vicki's cell phone rang just as she was pulling away from the curb. She stopped to answer it.

"Hi," said Dan's familiar voice. He was on duty for the first half of the day. "You guys coming?"

"We're on our way."

"Gideon's got the ponies here, at the north end of the field. Try to park close, because Krys gets as many rides as she wants."

Vicki laughed. "I'll try." After she disconnected, she twisted to look at Krys in her booster seat in the back. "That was Dan. The ponies are waiting for you."

Krys clapped her hands together and gave a little squeal of delight. "Oh, goody!"

All the traffic was moving in the direction of the fairgrounds, if you could call them that. It was a big vacant lot just to the west of town, on the north side of the train tracks. Bleachers had been hastily assembled, probably for the rodeo later, and plenty of folding tables had been set up beneath canopies. Just to the west of the booths a carnival had risen almost overnight, and the Ferris wheel was already spinning slowly. To the north side of that were some ramshackle lean-tos that Vicki assumed held prize livestock hoping for blue ribbons.

The fair wasn't huge, but it was big enough. An afternoon might be sufficient for an adult, but for Krystal it might be too much to do. A man in a reflective vest, holding an orange-coned flashlight, directed her toward a row of parked cars. She slipped into place and turned off the ignition. They'd arrived.

Overhead, a blindingly blue sky held only a few puffy clouds, what a pilot she had once known called "popcorn clouds." Rain later? Well, now was not the time to wonder.

She helped Krys out of her booster seat. "Now remember, don't let go of my hand and don't wander away from me."

"I won't." But Krys's eyes were already on the delights awaiting her, her head full of excited anticipation.

"Krys," Vicki said firmly.

The girl looked at her.

"Rules?"

"Hold your hand and don't go away from you."

Satisfied, Vicki locked the car and held out her hand. Krystal took it and skipped alongside her.

"What first?" Vicki asked as they approached the gate, even though she already knew the answer.

"Ponies!"

She laughed. As they reached the gate, she saw a face that had become familiar from somewhere. "Howdy," the man said. "You're Vicki Templeton?"

"Yes, I am, and this is my daughter, Krys. And you are?"

"Jake Madison, sometimes chief of police. We met when you were out walking with Dan. Right now I'm temporary ticket-seller extraordinaire. Make sure you come by the sheds to see my prize Angus." He winked. "She'll be heartbroken if you don't." Then he reached into his hip pocket and pulled out a white envelope. "Dan Casey left this for you. Come on in. Your entrance is already paid."

Once they passed the gate, Vicki looked in the envelope. "Oh, my!"

"What, Mommy?" Krys asked, tugging impatiently at her hand.

"Dan left us tickets for everything. All the rides, the rodeo..."

"Cool. Can we see the ponies now?"

Vicki looked around, trying to locate them. The north side, Dan had said.

Jake called out. She turned and he pointed. "Dan said ponies first."

Vicki had to laugh. An orchestrated day at the fair, and she didn't feel at all suffocated. She tucked the envelope full of tickets into her old fanny pack, which she wore around front so she could get to it, and the two of them set off.

The dry grass, already fairly well crushed even though it was still early, crunched beneath her feet. Tinny, cheerful music issued from loudspeakers on poles. The narrow paths between booths weren't overly full of people yet, but everyone nodded and smiled, and she returned the greetings. She found the booth to leave the flyers for Lena's garage sale, and the two women there oohed over Krys, who kept impatiently pulling Vicki toward the ponies.

Little kids bounced along like balloons that were barely tethered to the ground. Older kids wandered in small groups, most of them eating something, most of it food on a stick. Everything looked deep-fried one way or another. The only thing Vicki didn't see were the deep-fried turkey legs that were a staple at home.

At home. She caught herself. This was their home now.

They found the ponies without any trouble. A rope corral strung from metal posts contained four Shetlands, all saddled and ready, and tethered to the rope.

A strongly built man sat in a folding chair nearby, wearing jeans, cowboy boots, a plain Western shirt and a battered cowboy hat. He stood as they approached, and smiled. Very definitely Native American, he had his long black hair caught in a thong at the nape of his neck.

"Gideon Ironheart," he said, holding out his hand and shaking Vicki's. "The Templetons?"

"That's us." Vicki smiled. "I'm Vicki and—"

"I'm Krys," the little girl announced, bouncing on her toes. "These are real ponies?"

Gideon squatted to her eye level. "They sure are. Just about your size. What do you think?"

Krys studied them. "They're not too big."

"That's why I brought them. Smaller people can get afraid of the big horses. I know dogs that are bigger than my Shetlands."

Krys giggled. "You're teasing me."

"Not really." But he winked. "Wanna take a ride?"

Oh, yes, she did. Gideon helped her into one of the miniature saddles, adjusting the stirrups for her, showing her how she should press her feet into them. He kept up a patter the whole time, telling her the horse was called Belle, and her favorite thing in the whole world was a carrot.

Vicki realized her cheeks hurt from grinning so widely. She couldn't remember having felt this good in a long time, and she just loved watching Krys have so much fun.

"The pony ride's a success, huh?"

She turned her head to see Dan standing beside her. Everything inside her lurched when she saw he was in full uniform, gun on his hip. A tan deputy's uniform was different from the Austin PD's blue, but not different enough. It reminded her sharply that this man lived a life she wanted no part of ever again. But even as fear tugged her in one direction, attraction pulled her in a very different one. The man could have posed for a movie poster. Male to the last inch of him.

He'd been watching Krystal and smiling, but he looked at her when she didn't answer immediately.

"Yes," she said, finding her voice. "She's loving it. I can't thank you enough for all of this, including all the tickets. You didn't have to do that."

"No, I didn't. I wanted to. Some dreams just need to come true. Are you taking pictures? Because you'll never again see your four-year-old taking her first pony ride. I've got to keep circulating, but I'll be done early this afternoon. I hope I catch up to you."

He nodded and moved on, leaving Vicki with the feeling she needed to catch her breath. She pulled her cell phone out of her fanny pack and snapped some photos of Krys as Gideon led her on horseback around the small corral. Her daughter, who had appeared nervous at first, had now relaxed and was enjoying repeated turns around the small corral.

Other little kids were beginning to line up for rides, too, and soon two tall teenage boys appeared. One glance at them said they were related to Gideon. Soon other children were mounted and riding around, led by the boys.

And soon enough Krys's first pony ride came to an end.

By early afternoon, Krys seemed worn out by all the stimulation. There had been rides that had left her shrieking with delight, stops to play various games. She'd had her face painted, and taken another ride on the ponies, and now even Vicki was starting to forget everything they'd done. She finally found them some food that wasn't deep-fried, and a place at a picnic table under a canopy. Since the girl had been running at full tilt since she'd awakened that morning at six, Vicki was concerned that she needed a rest break. Krys was eager to eat her nachos and chili, and kept worrying that her face paint would disappear.

"If it does, we'll go get some more."

That settled her, and she dived into her meal with all the energy and concentration she'd expended on every one of her new experiences that day.

The breeze felt good to Vicki, as did the shade. Being from Austin, she was used to a more brutal sun, but that didn't mean she never wanted to escape it. Probably time to put on more sunscreen, too.

"Hi, ladies." Dan approached smiling, still in uniform. Despite her reaction to the fact, Vicki couldn't help noticing how well he filled it out. A powerful figure of a man.

Vicki managed to smile back despite wishing he

could change into civvies. Inwardly, she scolded herself, though. This was the same man who was becoming a friend to her and her daughter, and no uniform could change that. But her reaction to it told her she had some serious thinking to do.

Maybe she had moved Dan into a different category without realizing it. Maybe she had successfully managed to forget what he did for a living. Nothing else could explain her earlier reaction to seeing him in uniform. It shouldn't have felt like such a shock.

He sat across from them with a paper plate full of various foods on sticks, and a stack of paper napkins. "Been having fun?" he asked.

"Yup," Krys answered, her mouth still full of nachos.

Dan looked at Vicki and she nodded, smiling. "We've been running ourselves ragged. I think we tried a little bit of almost everything."

"I still want my cotton candy," Krys announced.

"After lunch," Vicki promised.

"There are rules even at the fair," Dan remarked. He was grinning at Krys.

"And another pony ride," she said stoutly.

"If Mr. Gideon has time. Lots of other kids want pony rides, too," Vicki said.

"What about the rodeo?" Dan asked.

She hesitated. She liked rodeos well enough, although she preferred small local ones to the big affairs some places held, where everyone was a pro. But while she'd expressed interest, she'd begun to question whether it would be a good experience for Krys at her age. Remembering the tickets in the envelope, she knew Dan had bought them admission, and it would seem rude, but…

As Dan noticed her silence, his grin faded and his gray eyes caught hers. "There could be lots of reasons for skipping the rodeo," he said, barely audible over the endless music playing from speakers, and the crowd noises.

"Like someone being so young."

"Hadn't thought about that." He glanced toward Krys. "Is someone counting on it?"

Vicki shook her head. Her daughter hadn't said a word about going to the rodeo, probably because she had no idea what one was. Vicki had been thinking about it in odd moments throughout the morning, and wondering if it might scare or upset Krys. All those bucking horses and bulls, riders being thrown to the ground…how would she interpret that? And what if something went wrong?

"I always thought," Dan said, "that a rodeo was like waiting for an accident."

Vicki blinked. "You don't like them?"

"Not my most favorite thing. The cowboys around here like a chance to show off, and some are pretty good. Still not my favorite thing. I spend a lot of time wincing for other people."

That brought a laugh from her. "Good description." At least she knew now that he wouldn't be offended if they didn't go.

"Peggy!" Krystal nearly screamed in her delight. Dan rose to his feet to greet Janine and her daughter, and soon they were all seated around the same table.

"George couldn't make it." Janine screwed up her nose. "And Peggy couldn't wait for tomorrow. Lena's still working her garage sale? She ought to be able to close that down soon."

"Unless it's going well. Are you taking Peggy to the rodeo?"

Janine shook her head. "Absolutely not. Those idiots are welcome to break their necks to prove their machismo, but I don't have to watch. What are you guys doing this afternoon?"

"At least one more pony ride and cotton candy. Beyond that... I think we've done everything that Krystal wanted to."

Krystal and Peggy chattered happily to each other about the things they'd done. Vicki thought Dan had to be feeling like a fifth wheel. He sat there eating, occasionally smiling. For the first time, it struck Vicki that it couldn't be easy for him to see families when he had none of his own. He seemed to like kids, but he didn't have any. A wave of sadness washed over her. Life could be cruel sometimes. Terribly cruel.

When he spoke, it was to bid them farewell. "I've got to clock out and get home. I'm going to see how Lena's doing. You all have a great time."

Then Krystal said something that froze Vicki's breath in her chest.

"Don't leave, Dan." She turned toward him and threw her arms around him. "Don't leave."

That night, Vicki sat on the front porch swing. Krys had fallen into an exhausted sleep, and the only altercation they'd had was over the face paint. Finally, her daughter had agreed to having her face washed. Little was left anyway but a smear, and while Krys demanded they go back tomorrow for more, Vicki hadn't caved.

She probably would, though. Krys's words still rang loudly in her head. *Don't leave, Dan.*

Lena poked her head out. "Young or old, depending on how you look at things, I'm taking my weary butt to bed."

"It was a good garage sale." Lena had spoken about it at dinner.

"Better than I expected. People will probably be bringing trailers off and on for the next few weeks to pick up their purchases, but I've only got two unsold pieces. I'll probably donate them." Then Lena stepped out. "Are you okay, Vicki?"

"I'm fine. Chasing Krys today wore me out a bit. She was running on excitement. I was just trying to keep up."

Lena laughed. "Now you know why children are born to young people. She sure talked about it at dinner. Good night."

"Sleep well."

"No question of that," Lena answered, then disappeared inside.

With one leg curled under her, Vicki used her toe to push the swing gently. It was a beautiful night, cooling down rapidly, but she was learning. She'd brought an afghan to wrap herself in.

Twice since moving here, Krys had expressed the fear that someone was going to leave her. Vicki had been hoping her daughter didn't have much memory of her father's death, that she could move on more easily because she wouldn't remember much except what Vicki told her.

But apparently, emotional connections ran deeper

than memory, and this move might have reawakened a fear that Krys hadn't been able to express before.

Vicki heard a sound and looked next door, to see Dan step out onto his own porch. His house was smaller than Lena's, but it had been built when every house had a porch.

Evidently, he heard the swing creaking, because he turned toward her.

"Beautiful night," he said.

"It sure is."

"Do you want company or solitude?"

She bit her lip, then realized she didn't want to be alone, even if they didn't speak a word. "There's room on the swing."

He crossed the yards and sat beside her on the swing. It shifted a little beneath his weight, then he started pushing them gently, giving her a break. "Krys seemed to have a great time today."

"She sure did. She wants to go back tomorrow. She's mad that we had to wash off the face paint."

He laughed quietly. "As I recall, there wasn't much left."

"Nope."

"Are you taking her?"

"I haven't decided yet. She wants another pony ride, too. I'm in one of those mixed-up-mother states. The fair only comes once a year, she'll only be four once, but I don't want to spoil her."

He sighed. "I'm no help with that. Utter lack of experience. One thought, though, if you won't be offended."

Vicki tensed a little. "Fire away."

"You matter, too. If you don't want to go tomorrow, you shouldn't have to. Just sayin'."

It was true. "I just don't know. I look back over the past year, and I wonder if I overcompensated with her."

"To some extent you probably had to. I mean, you became the only parent. But honestly, she doesn't strike me as a little tyrant, so whatever you did couldn't have been that bad."

"Thank you."

The swing continued to rock; the breeze ruffled the hair at the nape of Vicki's neck, chilling her a bit. She pulled the afghan up until she was wrapped to her chin.

Dan was a comfortable companion. Not in any way did he make her feel it was necessary to chat. The night's quiet settled into her, disturbed only rarely by a passing car.

"I had a great time today, too," she said after a while. "Thanks so much for the treat."

"My pleasure." He paused, then drove straight to the heart of her worry with unerring precision. "She's afraid of losing someone else, isn't she?"

"Oh, God." Vicki twisted until she could make out his profile, shadowy though it was beneath the porch roof. "You noticed."

"Kinda hard not to. Has she been doing a lot of that?"

"One other time, when we first got here. She asked me not to go away."

He swore quietly.

"My sentiments exactly. I guess Hal's death had a bigger impact than she showed before. Of course, it had to. I mean, her daddy never came home anymore. But after a few weeks she stopped asking, and seemed to accept it. Now this. I don't know if she's been feeling this all along and just didn't know how to tell me, or if this is something new because of the move. If it's the move, I'm going to hate myself."

Dan shifted closer until he could put an arm around her shoulders. "It's gotta be rough. I mean, does she even begin to understand death?"

"I don't think so. It's not that I didn't try. It's not that I didn't tell her he wouldn't be coming back, with all the sugarcoated stories about going home to heaven. I didn't lie to her, for heaven's sake!"

"I didn't think you had. It's just that she's so young. People my age have trouble comprehending it."

"Sorry," Vicki said. Dan's arm felt good around her, a friendly kind of support, and she needed support right now. She was truly worried about her daughter.

And about herself. Despite all her promises, she was letting another lawman into her life. Any convenient amnesia she had been suffering the past couple weeks had been broken by his appearance at the fair. A gun and a badge, two things that now had only bad associations for her.

"You know, I thought I got used to Hal being a cop. I lived in an alternate universe."

"Meaning?"

"Oh, I convinced myself that while bad things happened, they weren't going to happen to him. After all, most cops get to retirement without ever drawing their guns. Most never get hurt at all in any serious way. It was only when he got home and the relief washed through me that I realized how tense I'd been. How edgy."

Dan tightened his arm briefly, just briefly, but didn't

say anything. Letting her talk if she wanted to. He was good at that.

"If there's a level of denial deep enough, I never found it," she said slowly. "You *have* to believe that everything's going to be fine, but at some level you don't quite make it. Or at least I didn't."

"I pretty much went into denial for a while after we got Callie's diagnosis," Dan murmured. "Somehow we were going to cure her. I'm not sure I didn't make it harder on her. I didn't want to accept the truth. Sometimes that's a good thing, sometimes not."

"Yeah." Vicki hesitated, wondering how much closer she wanted to get to this man. Knowing more about him would probably make it worse, but she plunged in, anyway. He was her friend, after all, even if he could never be more than that. "It must have been just terrible, Dan."

"It was." A bald statement. "Took me a while to accept it. But eventually, I realized that even with all the anguish and pain at the end, I wouldn't have wanted to miss loving Callie."

"What are you saying?" Vicki felt a flicker of anger, as if he were scolding her in some way. She resented that. But his next words calmed her again.

"Only that I know how hard it is. We each have to find our own ways to cope. I found mine. You'll find yours. Maybe you have. And then there's Krystal. I can't imagine trying to do what you're doing. Just when life seems to freeze in a pain so consuming that all you want is to die, you have to live for someone else. Put on a good face. Be upbeat. At least I got to wallow for a while."

"Did wallowing help?"

"I don't know. I just did it. Hid in the apartment, neglected to take care of myself, damn near a cliché." He laughed quietly. "I look back at it now and wonder if I was doing what I thought I should be doing. Who knows? I just know that for a while I'd wake up, turn over, see the bed beside me empty, and I'd pound the pillow, hating the fact that I had to face another day. It was hard on the pillows."

Vicki couldn't help herself, because she felt her heart reach out to his pain, the same pain she had known. She leaned into him a bit and rested her head in the hollow of his shoulder. His arm around her tightened a little, like a hug. Nothing to alarm her.

"I pounded a few pillows, too," she told him. "Once— and I'm ashamed to admit this—while Krys was at day school, I stood in the kitchen and smashed every single dinner plate we'd gotten as wedding presents."

"Did it help?"

"Not a whole lot. I cussed myself out the whole time I cleaned up, worried that Krys might step on a pottery shard. When she came home that day, I was on my hands and knees using damp paper towels to be sure I got everything."

He squeezed her again. "Wow."

"Then I put on the bright face and we went out and bought new dishes. Very different ones. She was too young to even wonder about it. I did any number of stupid things at first. Well, they look stupid now. At the time I wasn't questioning myself very much. Maybe it was just expressing the inexpressible."

"Yeah. I hear you."

"And now this with Krys. Man, I hope it wasn't a stupid decision to move here."

"God, I hope not," he answered. Then, astonishing her, he caught her chin in his hand and tilted her face up. She looked at him in surprise, trying to read his shadowed face, wishing there was some light. But then he bent his head and kissed her.

This time it was no experimental touching of lips. This time his mouth was firm against hers, and when she didn't immediately resist, he ran his tongue across her lips, asking for entry.

She should have refused, but the fire he'd ignited with the first kissed leaped to renewed life, filling her with all the hungers and yearnings that life brought. She was alive. He was alive. Surely they were entitled to this little bit of pleasure?

His tongue dipped inside her mouth, teasing hers, learning her contours, finding ways to make shivers pass through her. Just a kiss, just a simple little kiss, but it seemed as momentous as a huge earthquake. She leaned into him, forgetting everything but the need he had awakened. She wanted him. If her arm hadn't been tangled in the afghan, she'd have wound it around his neck to pull him closer.

But then, with apparent reluctance, he withdrew. Vicki didn't want to open her eyes, didn't want reality to come crashing back. For just a minute, he had taught her that she could be free, alive and vibrant again.

He ran his fingertips lightly across her lips, then wrapped his other arm around her, holding her close as he pushed the swing to and fro.

"Now that," he said after a while, "was no experiment."

No, it hadn't been. The night seemed alive, suddenly, as if the darkness held promise. The whisper of the breeze in the trees felt like a song echoing the sensations he had evoked in her. Maybe he was the wrong guy, but it didn't matter. She'd just taken a step forward for the first time since Hal.

The front door opened slowly. Immediately, the two of them jerked apart.

"Mommy?" Krys sounded barely awake.

"I'm right here." She hoped her daughter didn't notice how breathless she sounded. "Do you need something?"

"You were gone." The answer that came was heart-wrenching. Bare feet padded on the wooden slats of the porch floor and soon the little girl in her nightgown stood in front of them. Before Vicki could move, Dan reached out and lifted Krystal, placing her between them. Vicki pulled the afghan free and wrapped it around her.

"You should be in bed, sweetie. I'm not going anywhere. Did you have a bad dream?"

"I dreamed a monster was chasing you."

Vicki stroked the girl's hair gently. "Well, you can see he didn't get me. Want me to put you back to bed?"

"No."

Vicki looked over Krys's head at Dan. He seemed to meet her gaze.

"That was a scary dream," he said. "We'll keep the monsters away, okay?"

Then, without a word, he wrapped mother and daughter in his arms and held them close. Krys snuggled right in, and the swing kept moving, rocking to and fro.

* * *

Reality was biting Vicki in the butt again. There was no longer any question in her mind that the move to Conard City had disturbed and awakened her daughter's deepest fears. Fears she had never expressed before. Maybe now she was old enough to speak them, but Vicki wondered just how much of a silent hell Krystal had been going through even as her mother had fought to make their days as normal as possible.

But what could she do now? Moving back to Austin would just create more problems. Krys was already attached to Dan, and Vicki felt uneasy about it. Dan was a neighbor. He might be around for a long time or he might choose to go away. He certainly wasn't bound to her daughter by anything except his friendship with Lena. And perhaps now by his friendship with Vicki.

Of all possible men for Krystal to attach herself to, she'd chosen the worst, a cop. A man who might go off to work one day and never return. God, what if Vicki had walked her daughter into another nightmare?

Krys had fallen asleep again, snuggled between the two of them.

Dan spoke, little more than a whisper. "Want me to carry her to bed?"

Vicki nearly refused, wanting him no more intimately involved with her or her daughter, but when she looked down, even in the poor light she could see that Krystal's hand had knotted itself into Dan's sweatshirt. Hanging on for dear life.

Whatever was going on here, she didn't want to make it worse. She looked at Dan and nodded.

He scooped the girl into his arms before he rose.

He didn't try to take the blanket away, but kept her bundled in it.

"Lead the way," he murmured.

Krys made a small noise but didn't wake, merely curled more tightly into Dan.

Vicki's heart felt as if it were being torn in two. The child's trust in him overwhelmed her and worried her. Maybe it was time to take Krys to a psychologist. She clearly had anxieties Vicki couldn't begin to imagine how to soothe.

Dan eased Krys down onto her bed, leaving her snuggled in the afghan. She sighed and rolled onto her side, sticking her thumb into her mouth.

"I can let myself out," he whispered.

"I need to lock up."

"I have a key." Surprising her, he pulled her into a quick, tight hug. "I'm off tomorrow. I'll see you."

Then he slipped from the room with amazing quiet for a man so big. Vicki sagged onto the Boston rocker, determined to be there if Krys woke again.

But it left her an awful lot of time to sit in the dark, pondering her past mistakes and wondering if she was making a bunch of new ones.

Nothing about life seemed simple anymore. Everything had turned into a tangle of potential complications. But maybe it had always been that way. Maybe before, she'd just been too happy and secure to notice it.

Still rocking, concerned about leaving Krystal alone, Vicki slowly fell asleep, remembering the peace of a group hug on the front porch swing.

Chapter Six

Sleeping in a hard wooden rocking chair all night left Vicki aching almost as soon as she stirred. Every muscle, every joint protested.

Then she heard voices downstairs: Kystal, Lena and Dan. Krystal mostly. Vicki recognized that tone. Her daughter wanted something. Vicki had to get down there before someone gave in to her.

When she stood, she groaned. Twisting and bending, she tried to ease the kinks out. What she needed more than anything was fresh clothes and a shower, but she decided that would have to wait. First she had to find out what was up with Krys.

Good heavens, it was already past nine. The alarm clock beside Krys's bed scolded her. She must have been more tired than she realized. Whatever, she had to get downstairs now, even if she looked like a witch, with tangled hair and rumpled clothes. Some things couldn't wait, primarily a four-year-old who sounded like she was on a campaign.

Vicki reached the bottom of the stairs in time to hear Dan say, "That's up to your mother, Krys. She's in charge."

Thank goodness for that, Vicki thought, feeling a flicker of amusement. She paused long enough to gather her hair into a tighter ponytail and rub some of the sleep out of her eyes. Then she walked into the kitchen, to find Dan, Lena and Krys gathered around the big round table having breakfast.

"Good morning," the two adults said.

Krys chirped, "Hi, Mommy."

Vicki returned the greetings while she poured herself some coffee. Dan pulled out a chair for her. Today's breakfast seemed to be sweet rolls from a bakery, Krys's inevitable Cheerios and milk. Krys had a mustache from the milk, but no one seemed to care.

"I must look awful," Vicki remarked. "I need a shower and a change."

"We'll forgive you," Lena said. "You want something else to eat?"

"This is fine." Finally, she glanced at Dan and saw him smiling as he looked at Krys. Vicki sensed he was enjoying something.

But all of a sudden she remembered their kiss and hug last night on the porch swing, and both warmth and desire washed through her. The man had given her and her daughter comfort, but he'd also given her something else. She wasn't sure that was a good thing.

"I'm not s'posed to bug you," Krys said, a bit of milk dripping from her chin. "Dan said."

Vicki propped her own chin on her palm. "But you're going to be a little bug, anyway."

Krys grinned.

With her free hand, Vicki grabbed a napkin and wiped her daughter's mouth and chin. "Next time you do the wiping."

"'Kay."

"So were you bugging Aunt Lena and Dan?"

Another grin, but no answer. Vicki looked at Dan and Lena. "Well?"

"She wants to go to the fair again today," Lena said.

"Pony rides," Dan added. "Oh, and face paint."

"I see." Vicki looked at her daughter. "You had that much fun, kiddo?"

"Yup."

Vicki could almost see the desire to plead written all over the girl's face, but so far she was heeding Dan's stricture not to bug her mother. Interesting. The child must be ready to explode.

Vicki pretended to think about it, although in truth she was going to say yes. Krys had enjoyed it, the fair wouldn't happen again for a year, and it seemed churlish to deny her. "First," she said finally, "I need to take a shower and change. That rocking chair was *not* a comfortable bed."

Krys surprised her. Milky mouth and all, she jumped down from her chair, then wormed her way onto Vicki's lap. "You stayed," she said simply.

"Yes." Vicki barely got the simple word out as her throat tightened painfully and a weight seemed to settle in her chest. *So many kinds of sorrow,* she thought helplessly. Maybe the biggest one now evidenced in Krys's insecurity.

Bowing her head, she pressed her face into Krys's silky hair, inhaling her daughter's wonderful, familiar scent, hugging her tightly. "Do you wish we'd stayed in Austin?"

"No!"

The vehemence of the answer surprised Vicki. She looked down and Krystal looked up at her. "I like it here."

Well, of course, she thought, as Krystal slid off her lap and went back to eating her cereal. Dan and Peggy and Lena and the fair…it seemed her daughter was sprouting new connections rapidly. But still, she had climbed out of bed from a nightmare that something was chasing her mother.

Sipping her coffee, Vicki watched her daughter eat, once again amazed by the complexity of a young child. Finally, she ate a piece of roll to tide her over, and excused herself to go clean up.

The shower washed away the last stiffness from her body. For the first time in forever, she didn't try to brush the curls out of her dark hair. Let them come. It would probably look like a wild cloud, and she was overdue for a cut, but today she just decided to let it do its own thing.

Another step, she thought as she once again dressed in jeans, and a lightweight, blue polo shirt. At least her Austin casual clothes fit in here. Soon it would be time to think about getting some serious winter clothing, she supposed. While they had an occasional touch of winter in Austin, she was certain it was nothing like Wyoming.

Random thoughts flitted around in her head, a break from more serious occupations. She must need it.

Downstairs she found Krys, who had dressed herself in her favorite T-shirt and jeans, with pink running shoes, practically bouncing up and down in her excitement. Lena appeared ready to go with them, and she remarked, "Dan's going to meet us there."

Well, well, Vicki thought sourly. *One big happy family outing.* Shame filled her an instant later. She really had to do something about her resistance to friendship. All Hal's friends had ever tried to do was help in every way that they could think of, and if it had overwhelmed her, maybe she should have found a way to let them know that she needed space, rather than running away.

But run away she had. Now she was here, and trying to fall back into her old habitual thinking. She looked at Krys as she put her in her booster seat, and wondered if she needed a mental health check. She'd run, claiming she felt smothered, and had perhaps caused her daughter more problems. Moving hadn't sound like such a bad thing when she had justified it, including thoughts of Krys that had always ended with *Well, she's so young.*

"Yeah," Vicki muttered to herself. Maybe she had utterly misjudged how much more secure her daughter might have felt in familiar surroundings. She guessed now she had a whole load of new guilt to live with, because she couldn't take back her decision.

"Mommy?"

She finished buckling the harness and looked at Krys. "What, honey?"

"You sound grumpy."

Caught, Vicki almost colored. "I'm a little mad at myself," she admitted.

Krys touched her cheek with small, soft fingers. "Don't be mad, Mommy. This is fun."

Wisdom from a child, Vicki thought, as she climbed in behind the wheel. Lena was already in the passenger seat.

"Maybe you need to talk a bit later," Lena remarked casually. "Been getting that feeling. I'm available. So's Dan if you want a man's perspective. Although to my way of thinking, us gals do a better a job of the thinking part."

A small laugh escaped Vicki. "Maybe so."

As it was Sunday morning, the fair wasn't as crowded yet as yesterday. Most people were probably in church, Vicki thought, and knew another pang of guilt. That was something else she'd let slip since Hal. It might be good for Krys, the nursery school, the Bible school classes. Or then again...

"You went away again," Lena said as they walked toward the ponies. "What's going on?"

Vicki took the safe path. "Just wondering about church around here. I haven't taken Krys in a long time. Would you recommend one?"

"Good Shepherd," Lena answered promptly. "Good pastor, nice folks for the most part. Great children's programs from what I hear. But don't be rushing into it."

Vicki, whose arm was swinging as Krys hung on to her hand and skipped beside her, looked at her aunt. "Are you trying to say something?"

Lena snorted. "Not in front of the girl. You may not approve of my heretical notions."

That surprised a laugh from Vicki and she let the subject go.

Gideon Ironheart was there with his ponies and welcomed them warmly. Then he introduced them to a teenage girl. "Kiana, my daughter. Took me a while to get her away from her swords and sorcery games."

Kiana, who had long, inky hair and beautiful dark eyes, laughed and gave him a shove on his shoulder. "I'm only impossible part of the time, Dad."

Gideon's eyes crinkled as he looked at Vicki. "She takes after her mother."

"Like you're easy?" Kiana asked. She squatted down and held out her hand. "You must be Krystal? That's such a pretty name. My dad says you liked Belle a whole lot yesterday. Wanna feed her a carrot?"

Krys, her eyes huge, nodded. She took Kiana's hand and let herself be led over to the string of ponies.

"Break out that camera, Vicki," Lena said.

Vicki was already reaching for it. Any nervousness she might have been feeling vanished the instant the pony snatched the carrot from Krys's tiny hand and the girl laughed with sheer delight. Kiana then showed her how to pet the horse, and soon it was clear Krys felt she'd made a friend for life.

Kiana seemed endowed with amazing patience for someone her age. She walked the horse and Krys around the small corral countless times, all the while chatting with her about horses and how she could come up to the ranch anytime Kiana was home and Vicki could bring her. The teen talked about the dozens of horses her dad had, and all the work involved in caring for them. "They say," she told Krys, "that my dad is a horse whisperer."

"What's that?"

"He speaks in a way the horses understand."

"Oh, I wanna hear!"

"It's not something you hear," Kiana said. "I'll get Dad to show you someday."

"My daddy's dead."

Silence ensued. Vicki's heart plunged so fast she felt as if she were in free fall. A strong hand gripped her elbow and it was a moment before she realized Dan had joined them. "Easy," he murmured. "Take it easy."

Vicki didn't know what else she could do. If Krys had mentioned it, then she'd needed to say it. Everything now depended on a girl who couldn't be more than sixteen.

"I'm sorry," Kiana said. "You miss him?"

"I have his picture in my playroom."

"That's good," Kiana replied.

"He sees me," Krys said with absolute certainty. "Is Belle sleepy?"

"Not yet. Are you?"

"Nope." Another word she had learned from Peggy. "I like this lots!"

"Belle likes little girls like you, too. When I was smaller, she was my favorite. Now I have to ride bigger horses."

Finally, Kiana called a halt, explaining that she didn't want Krys to get saddle sore. Then she had to explain what that meant. "You won't be able to sit down for a few days."

The thought made Krystal giggle, and she accepted that her ride had come to an end. They moved on, with an invitation from Gideon and his daughter to come up to the ranch soon. That seemed to thrill Krys, who announced in no uncertain terms that she wanted to see bigger horses.

More people were arriving, and tempting smells were issuing from a lot of the food booths. Silence had fallen over the three adults, but Krystal skipped merrily along, hunting for the face painter. When they reached the booth, her face sagged. "She's gone!"

"Maybe she's just late," Dan said. "A lot of people come late on Sunday. Are you hungry? Because I sure am."

Vicki's stomach growled as if in answer, making everyone, including her daughter, laugh. "I guess I am," she said, laughing at herself and shrugging.

"Well," said Lena, "there are two good reasons to ignore a diet. This is one of them. Let's go stock up on all the fat we can find."

"What's the other one?" Krys asked.

"To break a diet? Holidays, like Christmas and Thanksgiving."

Krys slipped her hand into Lena's. "Can I pick?"

"Anything you want."

Dan, walking beside Vicki, said, "You weren't really thinking you could feed her fiber and low-fat, were you?"

Vicki had to laugh again. "I don't do that to her. Balance is my goal. No balance today, I guess."

Krys got the corn dog she'd wanted the previous day, and a deep-fried pastry that was loaded with powdered sugar. Vicki gave in and had a corn dog, too. Dan once again filled a plate with a variety of fried foods, and Lena chose a big order of fries. "Fried in lard," she said with satisfaction.

At long last, Vicki allowed herself to really look

at Dan. She'd been avoiding it since he'd gripped her elbow, but as the four of them sat at a picnic table, there was no way to avoid it any longer. Out of uniform today, he looked amazing in a blue chambray shirt that stretched across his broad shoulders. A cowboy hat, clearly one that had seen a lot of use, was tipped back on his head. Behind the table, his narrow hips were concealed, but Vicki couldn't help remembering them, anyway. If ever a man had been built for jeans, it was Dan Casey.

Without realizing it, she slipped into a dreamy state of mind, into a place where she and Dan were alone, where everything else had ceased to exist. Absently, her eyes wandered his face, remembering how his lips had felt on hers, how his arms had felt around her. Her whole body craved a repetition, and finally she closed her eyes, letting the anticipation and hunger fill her. Why not? At the moment she was safe, and daydreaming wasn't a crime.

"…in Denver."

Abruptly, before her daydream could turn her into a torch, Vicki snapped back into the conversation. "Denver?" she repeated.

"You're falling asleep there, Vicki," Lena remarked. "Do we need to get you home?"

"Face painting," Vicki said automatically. "Not before that. You said something about Denver?"

"It's that time of year," Lena explained. "The girls and I go on our big shopping trip, take in a play or a concert. Which reminds me, we're playing bridge tonight. You want to join us?"

Vicki shook her head. "Thanks, but I'm not much into cards. When are you going?"

"Next weekend. Everybody—well, except me, of course—ditches their husbands and we have a hen party. Maybe when Krys is a little older you can join us." Lena laughed. "By then you'll be eager to see a city again."

Vicki managed a laugh, but she felt strangely disoriented. Lena was going away for a weekend. Why should that bother her? What was going on inside her?

Then her gaze leaped across the table. Dan was looking toward Lena, for which Vicki was grateful, because she feared what he might see on her face in that instant. Lena was going away. That meant her chaperone would be gone.

Only then did she realize how much she was relying on Lena to keep her safe from temptation.

Vicki looked down at her plate and decided that she really, *really* needed to get her head straight. Any more self-delusion might get her into serious trouble.

Daydreaming about a man in a dangerous profession, and then expecting her aunt's presence to protect her from her foolishness? Oh, boy. She'd been in a cocoon too long. She was a grown woman and needed to deal better than this.

Krys put an end to her soul-searching. "I want my face painted now."

Vicki looked at her half-eaten corn dog and knew she couldn't swallow another mouthful. "Let's go, then, kiddo. Aunt Lena and Dan can catch up when they're done."

Escape. Right then she needed it.

The following Friday night, Lena left for her bridge game about five thirty. "Call me if you need anything," she said as she prepared to go. "I'll try to be back before eleven."

"Take your time and have fun."

"We will. A bunch of husbands have probably already headed for Mahoney's Bar." She laughed as she walked out.

Vicki had been looking forward to an evening alone with Krys. While she enjoyed sharing the house with Lena, it had seriously cut into their mother-daughter alone time. Early morning over breakfast, weeknights when they'd spent hours playing games or just watching TV. Admittedly, there hadn't been a whole lot of that, thanks to Hal's friends, but there had been more of it when she was living alone with her daughter.

But almost as soon as Lena was gone, Vicki realized how big and empty the house felt now, even with Krystal's energy practically filling the place.

"Should we go for a walk?" she asked. Bedtime seemed out of the question if the girl didn't slow down a bit.

"'Kay," Krys answered.

Hand in hand, they started down the sidewalk, bathed in the pleasant summer evening that lasted so much longer here. "Let's practice crossing streets," Vicki suggested.

Krys grinned up at her. Wired or not, the girl seemed happier since the fair. Vicki's heart settled a bit and she gave her daughter's hand a squeeze. It was going to be all right.

Dan, wearing a long-sleeved gray shirt, jeans and jogging shoes, was sitting on his own front porch, doing some heavy thinking, one foot propped against the porch rail.

He saw Krys and Vicki walk away down the tree-lined street. They made a cute pair, Vicki wearing a lavender T-shirt and jeans, and Krys skipping along beside her in the pink that appeared to be her favorite color. They hadn't glanced in his direction, and for some reason he'd failed to call out a friendly greeting.

Of course, he'd been trying to keep a low profile since the fair. He wasn't a dunce. As a cop he'd gotten really good at reading people, and he'd picked up on cues that Vicki wasn't entirely comfortable with the amount of time he spent around her and her daughter.

He understood. He was a cop, after all, and he hadn't missed Vicki's startled reaction when she'd seen him in full uniform last Saturday at the fair. Bad reminders. And from what she'd said about being afraid every time her husband had gone out the door, Dan got it.

He idly wondered if telling her that a cop was three times more likely to be struck by lightning than killed on the job would help her relax, then decided little could probably do that in the wake of Hal's death. Availability bias. He'd studied it in one of his college classes. She was seeing the whole world now through a single incident. As for whether her fears all along had been as great as she'd said, or amplified by Hal's murder, there was no way to know.

He had known cops who thought they were in danger every time they went on duty. They expected it. Funny thing was, expecting it seemed to cause it. Yet some recent stats he'd read said about 90 percent of cops retired without ever having fired their guns except on the practice range. He'd likely be one of them.

He sighed, and knew he was having a pointless argument with himself, because he doubted any of that would persuade Vicki. He didn't see his job as at all dangerous. Domestics were the only time he got edgy. But how he felt about it couldn't change the way Vicki felt.

Feelings were immutable things. Burned deep, they guided actions more than thought. You sure as hell couldn't reason with a feeling, no matter how hard you might try.

Which was part of what was giving him a problem. His feelings for Vicki were going places he was sure she didn't want. He should never have kissed her. Doing so had started a wildfire in him that wouldn't listen to his brain. He wanted that woman. He liked that woman. As for her daughter…well, he was fast coming to love that little girl. It was far too easy to imagine a future that contained both of them.

His foolishness almost amused him. He wasn't usually a foolish man, although like everyone else, he had his moments.

So he'd been staying away to give Vicki the space she seemed to want, and to avoid enhancing Krystal's attachment to him. That, too, had caused concern to flicker over Vicki's face a time or two. The woman was under enough stress with just the move. She didn't need to be wondering if her daughter was growing too close to a man she didn't want to become a permanent fixture.

Dang! The spinning of his own thoughts was growing frustrating. It should be so simple. Dan wanted the woman, and if something grew between them, he'd gladly welcome her daughter, too. No problem there.

Except Vicki. He knew damn well she wanted him, too, but she was afraid of it. Kinda turned things into an emotional time bomb.

But Vicki was creeping into his dreams, popping up in his thoughts without warning, and every time he thought about her he hardened a bit. Well, that wasn't enough for the long term.

Staying away this week had been tough. It was not only putting a distance between him and Lena, but he found himself wondering every evening what Krys and Vicki were doing. Missing them.

So he was a damned fool. Fair enough. There ought to be some reasonable way to handle this that didn't involve avoiding the three of them entirely. Lena must be wondering what the devil was going on, and he prized her friendship.

At least he had a game to coach tomorrow. That would help. And two nights this week he'd had a game to play in. That helped, too. Maybe he needed to take up some additional sports. Bowling?

He could have laughed at himself. He liked bowling well enough, but not enough to commit to a team. Anyway, his schedule was often erratic. Hard enough to keep up with baseball and the soccer team he coached.

But he was aware of something else changing in him, too. He'd rather sit here on his front porch mooning over Vicki than go down to Mahoney's and join the others to watch a game and have a few beers. Oh, that was bad.

He waved absently as cars drove by, passed some idle words with his neighbors who were out strolling, but all that seemed to barely scrape his internal fascination with thinking about Vicki.

The street quieted down as twilight descended. Fewer cars, almost no people now. Everyone was headed home to spend the rest of the night with a book or the TV.

Which was what he ought to do, instead of trying to solve unsolvable problems.

Removing his foot from the porch railing, he stood, deciding to go inside and pick up that book he needed to finish. Some distraction would do him good.

"Dan!"

His hand had just reached for his door latch when he heard Krystal call out. He almost pretended not to hear her, but then he heard something else that made him pivot quickly.

It all happened so amazingly fast, but in that instant time seemed to slow to a crawl. The sound of a car coming way too fast. Vicki crying her daughter's name. Everything suddenly became acutely clear, from the deepening shadows, the car coming at a fast clip without headlights, the leafy trees motionless as if frozen.

The girl had slipped away from her mother and was running out into the street, heedless of the car. Vicki hit a dead run. So did Dan.

With horror, he saw Vicki trip over a tree root and land on the ground. Saw Krystal still running his way. Gauged the distance and started an almost incoherent prayer in his head as he hit top speed and ran into the street to grab the girl.

He got to her in the nick of time, grabbing her, tumbling to the ground and rolling away just as the car roared past, so close that he could feel its heat.

Krystal started crying. Vicki came running, screaming her daughter's name. The cop in Dan took a mental snapshot of the vehicle and driver. All in an instant. Then people began to pour out of their houses onto their porches.

He sat up with Krystal in his arms, hugging her so tightly that he might have scared her more. "It's okay," he heard himself say. His heart thundered like a galloping horse. Fury at the driver filled him, but his main concern was the sobbing little girl.

Then Vicki scooped her from his arms. "Are you all right? Is she okay?"

Dan rolled to his feet. "I think she's okay." He was fairly certain he'd protected her well enough. He suspected the same couldn't be said about himself. "Out of the street. Now."

The words penetrated Vicki's fear for her daughter, and she scurried with her over to the sidewalk in front of Lena's house. Only then did she set the girl on her feet, studying her anxiously.

Dan called out to the neighbors. "Everyone's okay, folks." They began trickling back inside, probably wondering what had just happened.

Vicki knelt in front of Krystal. "Does anything hurt, sweetie?"

"No." Krystal's sobs were turning into hiccups. "I was scared."

"Oh, baby, so was I."

"Get her inside and check her out. I'll be right there." Dan pulled out his cell phone, amazed he hadn't crushed it when he'd rolled with Krystal, and called the dispatcher. "Jay, Junior Casson just came speeding southbound down Collier at about fifty in a twenty-five. Nearly hit a little girl crossing the street. I want him picked up now."

* * *

Inside, he found Vicki and Krys sitting together on the couch. Vicki had protective arms wrapped around her daughter. Krys's tears were drying, but Vicki's face was still almost white. He squatted in front of them, noting that Vicki had a few small abrasions on her chin.

"How are you?" he asked her. "Did you get hurt when you fell?"

"I'm fine. Dan, I can't thank you enough..."

He shook his head. "Don't. I'm just glad I reached her." Then he looked at the girl. "What about you, pumpkin?"

Krys, who had been sucking her thumb again, pulled it out of her mouth. She wormed out of her mother's hold and landed between Dan's thighs to give him a big hug.

"Not mad at me?" he asked her.

"No. You helped me."

He stood up with the girl in his arms, feeling the adrenaline seeping away. With its departure came the awareness that he was probably growing some good bruises on his hip and shoulder. Turning, he sat beside Vicki on the couch, so the child was with them both.

At once Vicki reached out and drew her daughter close again. Dan forgot about everything that had been troubling him earlier, and wound his arms around both of them. For a long time nobody said a word.

"That guy was driving like a maniac," Vicki said eventually.

"They're going to pick him up. One nice thing about being a cop here. I recognized the idiot behind the wheel."

"Good." Although Vicki didn't sound as if satisfaction was going to ease her terror anytime soon. "Dan, if you hadn't…if…"

"Shh," he said gently. "No point worrying what didn't happen. I'm just glad I was there. Of course, if I hadn't been, Krys probably wouldn't have run into the street." And she'd have been less eager to see him if he hadn't been staying away. Guilt struck him, hard on the heels of fear for the child.

"Don't blame yourself. My God, you saved my daughter." Vicki made a choked sound. "Would you believe we'd been practicing how to properly cross streets while we were out walking?"

The irony didn't escape him.

"I was bad," Krys said. "Look both ways first."

Dan didn't have a clue how to respond to that. Saying she hadn't done anything wrong would be untruthful. Blaming it all on the driver would only be partially correct. He looked across the top of the soft blonde head cradled between them and met Vicki's gaze. She still appeared pinched, but a little less pale.

"That's right," she said. "Look both ways. Sometimes cars come really fast."

"Sorry."

Vicki sighed shakily. "It's good to be sorry, but it's even better not to do it again. Okay?"

"'Kay."

Her hand still trembled as she lifted it to stroke Krys's hair. She looked at Dan again. "What about you? Are you okay? That was a hard fall."

"Just a few bruises. I've rolled before."

"God, I never saw anybody run as fast as you did."

"You were doing a pretty good job yourself."

"I tripped." Anguish laced the words, and he watched as she drew a few deep, steadying breaths.

Dan wondered if they needed to change the subject, get her and Krys's mind off what had just happened. He doubted it would be as easy to make Vicki move past it quickly, but he wanted to see Krys smiling again. What had almost happened was probably meaningless to her, and a lot of her terror likely had come from being grabbed that way. It had probably conveyed more to her than the whole rest of the situation.

"How about I read a story," he said. "Or maybe we can play a game?"

"Game," said Krys promptly. She gave up sucking her thumb and wiggled free of the confinement of two hugs.

"Go get one, honey," Vicki said. From the expression on her face, Dan got the distinct feeling that letting her daughter out of her sight, even to run upstairs, was difficult right now. It might be difficult for a long time to come.

Vicki turned back to him after watching Krys disappear around the corner. "Dan, I've got to thank you—"

He shook his head, about to tell her it wasn't necessary. As if he was going to stand by and watch any child get hit by a car? But just then his cell rang. He rolled his eyes at Vicki, who smiled wanly.

It was Dispatch, of course. "Good. All right, I'll be in shortly, Jay." He disconnected and rose. "I'm sorry. They caught the driver, but by the time they did he'd slowed down to a legal speed. His dad's screaming they need to let him go, and while we could hold him for seventy-two hours without a charge, we don't do that around here for anything less than real mayhem. I've got to go in and file my report. Knowing that family, Junior will skip the county before morning."

Dan saw her face become pinched again. "I understand," she said, her voice muffled. Just then Krys bounced into the room carrying a board game.

"I'm sorry, Krys," he said. "I've got to go to work for a little while. We'll play tomorrow, okay?"

Krys's smile faded, but she nodded. "Will you come back?"

"I promise. If you're asleep, maybe your mommy will let me come up and peek in on you."

"Of course," Vicki said swiftly.

That brought the smile back to Krys's face. "Okay," she said. "Mommy can play with me."

From the look on the child's face, Dan figured she was going to fight sleep with all her might until he got back. He guessed he'd better hurry.

Chapter Seven

Dan filled out his incident report in record time, insisted that Junior's blood be tested for illicit substances, then raced back to Lena's house.

Sure enough, when he let himself in, Vicki was on the couch with Krys, and it was after ten. Way past the girl's bedtime. His heart squeezed with concern and caring for both of them. He was definitely in it up to his neck, and right now he didn't care.

"She wouldn't go to bed until you got back," Vicki said.

At the sound of her mother's voice, Krys stirred, opened her eyes and smiled. "Dan," she said with satisfaction.

He perched on the edge of the couch beside her. "Do you know the story of Cinderella? How her fairy godmother turned her pumpkin into a coach?"

"Yup," Krys said sleepily.

"And then if she didn't get home in time, it turned into a pumpkin again?"

Krys nodded.

"You're going to turn into a pumpkin if you don't get to bed soon."

A sleepy giggle emerged from Krys. "You called me a pumpkin before."

"And you're a very cute pumpkin. But you still need your sleep."

"Carry me?"

Dan quickly searched Vicki's face and she nodded. He scooped the girl up in his arms, suppressing a wince as he felt the bruise on his shoulder protest. Oh, it was going to be a good one. So was his hip, come to that.

Ignoring both, he carried his precious cargo upstairs, then said good-night and slipped out while Vicki got the girl into bed.

"Dan…" Vicki's voice trailed after him. "Stay a bit?"

"Sure."

Since he knew his way around Lena's house as well as he knew his own, he started a pot of coffee. It had almost finished brewing by the time Vicki appeared.

"That smells good," she remarked. She looked so weary it troubled him.

He was leaning back against the counter, waiting for the coffee, when she approached. "Turn around."

Surprised, he obeyed, then nearly jumped when she touched his shoulder, and he realized her fingertips met bare skin. Hunger surged in him.

"I didn't say anything before," she said. "I didn't

want Krys to notice. But your shirt's torn. Dan, that's an awful bruise you're getting."

"I'll survive." He felt frozen in place, wanting her touch to continue. But her fingertips went away.

She said, "I guess it's too late for ice."

"Probably. It'll be okay, Vicki. If that's the worst to come out of tonight, I'm grateful. I'm also grateful we got Junior Casson."

Dan heard her move to the table, so he turned around again.

"Is he a problem?" she asked.

"Wild child, although he's getting a little too old for that. Every place has a family or two like the Cassons, always on the edge of trouble, always creating it if they can't find it. Mostly stupidity and orneriness. Anyway, he's going to be off the streets for a little while, longer if we find out he was under the influence."

She nodded, then gave a start. "Let me get your coffee. You sit down. If your shoulder looks like that, other parts must hurt, too."

He eyed the hardwood chairs, gauged his hip and said, "Living room?"

"Fine by me. And for goodness' sake, if you want to use the recliner, use it."

He paused in the doorway. "I didn't want to take Hal's seat."

She sighed. "I kinda guessed. But Hal hasn't been using it. Make yourself comfortable. Please. If that was going to be a problem, I wouldn't have brought the sofa with me. I expect other people to use it."

So Dan risked taking the end of the sofa away from where she always perched, and accepted a mug of hot coffee gratefully. When she sat, she curled one leg under her, leaned back against the overstuffed arm and faced him, holding her own mug in both hands.

"This is going to be some story to tell Lena," she remarked.

"Wouldn't surprise me if she went down to the jail in the morning to give Junior a piece of her mind."

Vicki laughed quietly. "I wouldn't mind doing that myself."

"He's sure as hell going to get one from me. I'd have done it tonight except I got the feeling Krys wouldn't go to bed until I got back."

"You called that right." Vicki sipped coffee, then astonished him with what she said next. "You've been avoiding us. Did I do something wrong?"

Crap, he thought. *Called out*. He gave her points for it, though. Apparently, she was a lot like her aunt. "I got the feeling you didn't want me so involved with you and Krys." He could be blunt, too.

She nodded slowly, looking pensive. "I told you about my fears. But that doesn't mean we can't be friends. Krys really likes you. So do I, for that matter." Vicki's eyes lifted, meeting his. "We can do friends, right?"

It might be a new kind of hell, given how badly he wanted her, but he wasn't a proud man. He'd take what he could get. This past week of trying to do what he believed Vicki wanted had been a kind of hell, anyway. "Sure," he said. No point in being blunt about *this*. It was tough enough and he didn't want to bring her fears back.

"Good." She hesitated, then astonished him anew. "And do me a favor?"

"If I can."

"Next time you decide to read my mind, tell me what you think I'm thinking. You were the one who mentioned that silence leaves a lot of empty space to imagine things."

He laughed. Somehow he just had to. "Okay," he agreed. "So what *was* going on?"

"I was worried about Krys. She's said a few things, done a few things, that make me think she's having separation anxiety. I suspect the move was harder on her than I expected. And while I'm not sure she remembers Hal much, if at all, she's been through a lot of loss in little more than a year. Anyway, she's attached to you, obviously, and I don't mind. Honestly."

"Are you sure about that? I heard what you said about cops."

She bit her lip. "Okay, I'm a little worried. But it's crossed my mind that I can't protect against everything, and she has needs to be met. You're apparently meeting one, and I'd have to be a witch to deprive her."

He paused before responding carefully, "My job isn't all that dangerous, Vicki. I've been a deputy for seventeen years. Do you know how many times I've had to pull my gun? None."

"Really?" She hesitated. "I think Hal did a couple of times."

"Big cities are different. And I'm not saying it never happens around here, but it's been two decades since we lost a deputy. We have our share of problems, I won't deny it. But I think it's more dangerous to be a crab fisherman."

"Maybe so. Anyway, I don't need to pass my fears to Krys. She's struggling to make new connections here, and she needs every one of them."

He'd already figured out Vicki was remarkable in a lot of ways, but it floored him to see her put aside a very natural fear of her own in favor of what she believed to be her daughter's best interest. "So I'm not smothering you?"

Her expression turned wry. "To do that, you'd need to try a whole lot harder, cowboy."

He grinned. "Fair enough. I'm coaching girl's soccer tomorrow. The six-to-eight group. You wanna bring Krys to watch? There'll be some younger kids there watching, too."

"That'd be good for her," Vicki agreed.

"And what about you? What would be good for you?"

The question seemed to startle her, but before she could answer, the front door opened and Lena swept in. Clad in her usual Western shirt and jeans, her only concession to playing bridge with her girlfriends had been a dab of makeup.

"We slaughtered them," she said cheerfully. Then she took in the scene on the couch, and evidently something got her attention. "What happened? Is everything all right?"

"It is now," Vicki said. "I'll let Dan tell you. A cop can do it without breaking down."

Lena sat on the other sofa almost as if her strings had been cut. "Krys?"

"She's fine," Vicki said swiftly. "Thanks to Dan."

So he sketched what had happened, almost as if he were filling out a report, but adding a few details, such as how Vicki had tripped, and why her chin was abraded.

"Well, I never," Lena said. For a minute or so she

didn't say any more, then demanded, "Junior Casson? He's in the jail?"

"Yes," Dan answered.

"Shoulda let that young man run. Maybe he'd never come back." She shook her head. Then she took in Dan. "Are you all right, too?"

"Bruised but fine."

Lena rose. "I'm gonna get me some of that coffee— there's more, right?"

Vicki nodded.

"Good. I'm getting some, then you're going to take me through this again, Dan Casey. And this time not like an abbreviated police report."

He flashed a smile. "Yes, ma'am."

She was tutting as she walked out. "Junior Casson. I'm going to have some words for him."

The soccer game the next afternoon turned out to be a lot of fun for both Vicki and Krys. Krys soon met three children near her own age, and it provided a perfect entrée for Vicki to become acquainted with some of the other women. The young girls running wildly on the field, occasionally getting confused about where to go and what to do, provided an endless source of conversation and some amusement.

Mothers cheered loudly, but refrained from any critical remarks, which was a pleasant surprise for Vicki, who'd gone to some recreational league games with friends and discovered that some parents took the game as seriously as if it were the World Cup. The women surrounding her that afternoon remained a whole lot more laid-back, apparently thinking their children were here to have fun, not get college scholarships ten years down the road.

When it was over, Vicki was encouraged to come back next weekend, and even had an invitation to join a local church.

She had noted, however, that Dan seemed to be moving a bit stiffly and felt a pang for the discomfort he must be feeling. Her heart wanted to reach out to him even though it was nothing terribly obvious, but when they met up after the match, as the girls and their families scattered to cars or along the neighborhood sidewalks, she asked him about it.

"Just bruising, but I guess I got some road rash on my shoulder. My skin is annoyed with me." He smiled. "I'll be fine. Now how about I take us all for ice cream?"

"Yay!" Krys squealed. Then she added, "Mommy, I wanna play soccer."

Vicki opened her mouth to say she wasn't old enough yet, but Dan spoke first. "There's a group of four- and five-year-olds. One of the elementary school-teachers runs it as a kind of intro-to-skills group." He turned to Vicki. "And lest you worry, no heading of the ball allowed at that age." He chuckled. "Not that most of them are in any danger of getting their heads that close to a ball."

"Thanks. I'll check into it." She looked down at Krys. "We'll see what I can find out."

The ice cream parlor was just off the town's central square. Vicki was able to find parking nearby, and Dan almost as close. They met at the door and he ushered them in.

Retro would be a good word for the place's appearance. Vicki wondered if it just hadn't changed in fifty years or if it had been designed to look like something out of *Happy Days*. Most people were buying cones or cups and leaving with them, so the three of them found seats easily at the counter, which was where Krys wanted to sit, on a high stool. Vicki and Dan sat on either side of her, and Vicki helped her daughter read the menu. While the child did fairly well with simple children's books, the menu was full of a lot of words she had to sound out. Vicki was not surprised, however, when they got only partway through the listing and Krys made her decision.

"Chocolate with chocolate sprinkles."

"Cone or cup?"

Krys thought about it for a second. "Cone," she announced.

Dan ordered a double scoop of chocolate chip and Vicki a cup of frozen yogurt. She soon discovered why most people probably didn't stay here with their ice cream. Dan was greeted by everyone, while his ice cream began to melt down the cone into the napkin he'd wrapped around it. He introduced Vicki and Krys to all comers, which took a fair amount of time, as well.

He winked at Vicki over Krys's head. "Great place to have a meet-up."

"So it appears." Glancing down at Krys, Vicki saw fatigue beginning to appear. Her daughter had stayed up late last night, had gotten up early this morning filled with excitement about going to the soccer game, and had been running at full speed ever since. She was still enjoying her ice cream, licking round and round to make sure she caught all the drips, but she was slowing down.

Just then Dan's cell phone beeped. He shook his head a little and pulled it out, quickly scanning a text. "Gotta go. I'm sorry. Work. See you later?"

Vicki nodded, watching as he dropped a kiss on the top of Krys's head. "Later, pumpkin," he said, before hurrying out.

Vicki looked up from her ice cream at her mother. "He works a lot."

"Yes, he does." Apparently, around here hours weren't as regular for cops as they'd been in Austin. Smaller department, she decided. Sometimes they probably needed officers on call, more than she was used to. But really, she had little on which to base that. This might be unusual. Regardless, she somehow seemed to be getting in tune with his job and becoming more accepting of it.

"Mommy?"

"Yes, honey?"

"Wanna go home."

So, ice cream in hand, with plenty of napkins, they went out to the car and drove home. Krys kept up licking her ice cream until it was down inside the cone, but then she nodded off, just as they pulled into Lena's driveway.

Vicki climbed out and looked into the backseat. Krys was sound asleep, with the contents of the cone dribbling onto one of the napkins. Smiling, Vicki caressed her daughter's head gently, then grabbed the cone in a wad of napkins. She heard the front door and saw Lena come out.

"Need help?" her aunt asked.

"If you could grab the ice cream mess, I'll grab Krys."

Lena took the wad in both hands. "My, she's tuckered. Of course, she's been going like ninety."

Vicki laughed quietly, unbuckling her daughter, then lifting her out of the car. "That she has."

With her hip she shut the door, then used the auto-lock button on her keys and settled Krys more comfortably on her hip.

"You can just put her on the couch if you want," Lena said as they headed inside. "We can klatch in the kitchen."

"Sounds good to me. Dan had to run in to work. He said he'd be over later."

"'Bout time he started coming by again."

Krys stirred a little, her eyes fluttering open as Vicki laid her on the couch and spread an afghan over her.

"Mommy?"

"Sleep, little dove. I'll be in the kitchen."

Krys sighed, rolled over and stuck her thumb in her mouth. Evidently all the problems weren't gone yet.

Sitting at the kitchen table with Lena felt relaxing to Vicki. Her aunt was a good woman, always great to talk with about nearly anything. She might joke that book-keepers were boring, but she was a widely read woman who could discuss almost anything if she chose.

Her sights were set a little lower at the moment, however. She eyed Vicki with concern. "Are you all right? I can see that Krystal is, but you were the one who got the biggest shock last night."

"It rattled me a lot," Vicki admitted. "Right now, I don't want Krys out of my sight."

"We can move into the other room if you want. I

doubt the two of us talking will wake her. She's out like a light from what I saw."

"Yeah." Vicki stared down into her coffee cup. "You know, Lena, even with all that's happened, I don't think I've ever been as scared as I was last night. If not for Dan…" She could barely stand to think about it.

"A long time ago, I decided kids must all have guardian angels. How else do so many of them ever grow up?"

A weary laugh escaped Vicki. "She sure had one last night."

"And I'm mad at the jailers."

At that, Vicki lifted her head. "Why?"

"They wouldn't let me scold Junior Casson. Now I ask you, the man nearly kills my grandniece and one of my best friends, and if he doesn't want to see me I don't get to tell him off?"

Vicki's laugh came a little easier this time. "Dan may do it for you. He said he was going to give Junior a piece of his mind."

Lena ruminated a moment, then said, "He'll do a good job of it, too. I've heard him dress down some youths before. Junior will have no doubt that he's an idiot by the time Dan is done."

"Good."

Lena peered at her. "Did you sleep much last night?"

"Honestly? No. I kept seeing it over and over—Krys running into the street, me falling, Dan running faster than the wind. He barely made it, Lena. However casually he treats it, except for him…" The tears came then, running freely down her cheeks. A choked sob escaped her.

Lena jumped up and came to hug her tightly. "Let it out, girl. Let it out."

Vicki couldn't stop it. She'd remained calm for Krys's sake, but she couldn't do it another moment. Her daughter had come within a second of being run over by a car. The scene ran repeatedly in Vicki's head like a horror movie on infinite loop.

Lena patted her shoulder, made comforting sounds, but didn't do a thing to make Vicki feel she should stop crying. She'd lost her husband, and had just almost lost her daughter, and the pain surged in her, needing an outlet.

It took a long time, but finally she began to run out of tears. Her chest felt so tight she could hardly breathe, but finally she managed a ragged one. Lena straightened and passed her a fresh kitchen towel to wipe her face.

"Maybe you should take up kickboxing."

Startled, Vicki raised her head, holding a now damp towel. "What?"

"There must be enough rage in you to want to take on the universe sometimes. Pounding something might do you some good."

"I agree." The deep voice startled her even more and she swung her head around to see Dan standing in the doorway, arms folded, leaning against the jamb. "Sorry, I let myself in. If I should go, tell me."

She didn't want him to go, although she was sorry he'd seen her such a mess. But then she remembered he'd lost his wife. He was probably as familiar with her reaction as anyone could be.

"Stay," she said, her voice still hoarse from crying.

He came into the room, poured a coffee and joined

the women at the table. "There was a spell after Callie died that I went to the gym nearly every day just to pound the punching bag until I couldn't punch it anymore."

"Did it help?"

He tilted his head. "I don't know that anything really helps. But it sure does wear you out. So the anger gets expended, and the grief moves back in, until the next time anger takes over." He shrugged his uninjured shoulder. "It eases, Vicki. That's all I can say."

Silence fell. When Vicki at last reached for her cup to moisten her throat, she found the coffee had grown cold. The instant she stirred as if to rise, Lena snatched the mug, emptied it in the sink and refilled it.

"Thank you."

Lena smiled sadly at her. "I can't do much else except keep the coffee coming."

Vicki reached out to squeeze her aunt's hand. "You've done a whole lot for Krys and me. A whole lot."

"Time will tell." She turned her attention to Dan. "So did you give Junior a piece of my mind for me?"

"Yeah, I did," he said. "And a piece of mine, as well. Sorry you couldn't do it yourself. I know you'd have felt better."

"I feel good enough that you did it."

"First he was angry, but I just kept at him, Lena. You know how stubborn I can get."

"Pretty stern, too," she agreed.

"By the time I was done I saw something I thought I'd never see on a Casson face—shame. Doubt it'll last, though."

"How long will he get?"

"I don't know. A lot depends on whether he was

under the influence. As it is, reckless endangerment carries a decent sentence. Maybe assault with a deadly weapon. It's up to the county prosecutor now. We'll see."

"If the county attorney feels like most of us in this county, she'll throw the book at him," Lena said. "About time a Casson got sent away for a while."

A quiet laugh escaped Dan. "He's going to have trouble finding a sympathetic jury, that's for sure."

Vicki was only half attending to the conversation as she waited for her emotional storm to settle completely. All she had to do, all she ever had to do, was take one step at a time. Then the next. Since Hal's death, looking too far forward occasionally daunted her, and right now she wasn't the least interested how long Junior Casson spent in jail. It was enough that he'd been caught.

What mattered was that her daughter was all right. Vicki wasn't feeling especially vengeful, although she might later. Right now she was absorbing the fact that she had something to be truly grateful for. Krystal was fine, apparently less disturbed by last night than anyone else.

Vicki closed her eyes a moment, accepting a quiet sense of blessing, a blessing that existed because of Dan. She opened her eyes and looked at him, to find him regarding her with concern.

"Thank you," she said again. "And don't tell me I don't need to thank you. I do."

He nodded once, saying nothing, his gaze steady.

He was a remarkable man. Handsome, of course. She liked the way time and the sun had put fine lines around the corners of his eyes, lines that crinkled when he smiled. She liked the warmth she almost always saw in his gray eyes. She liked the way he treated Krys, and with the passage of time she had stopped worrying that he might overstep with her daughter. He never did, and the more he became involved, the more comfortable Vicki felt. He had good instincts, and she didn't mind it when he made a suggestion. Not now. She no longer feared him encroaching.

He was very different from Hal. She had loved Hal with her whole heart, but he'd been a different man, more excitable, more hyperkinetic. Everything about Dan created a calming atmosphere, which she appreciated.

Well, except for her attraction to him. Traitorously, it was rising in her again, the longing for another kiss, for more than a kiss. She looked quickly away for fear he might read her reaction.

How could she be feeling such things hard on the heels of her near breakdown? It seemed impossible and made her feel both guilt and shame. But as soon as she recognized it, she caught herself. It was simply a sign that she was still alive. And like it or not, she was very much alive.

Just pass it off as life trying to reassert itself. That was inevitable, and it was surely no crime.

The conversation between Lena and Dan flowed into slower, easier channels. Lena asked about soccer practice, then talked about her plans with her friends the coming weekend.

"I'm going to spend more than I should, eat more than I should, and laugh until my ribs hurt," she told them. "Say, Dan, aren't you about due for vacation again?"

"Yeah, but I'm waiting. I always go in August or September, and I decided this year to take a winter vacation."

Lena cocked a brow. "Heading for the sun?"

"I don't know. I haven't been skiing in a while, and I was thinking about that."

Lena snorted. "Talk about spending more than you can afford!"

Dan laughed. He glanced at Vicki, but didn't make any effort to get her to talk. Nor did she feel any desire to. It was enough to ride the flow of their conversation while matters inside her tried to settle. All the changes, especially Dan and last night, had altered her internal landscape. It might take a while for her to become comfortable inside her own skin again.

"I think I'm going to run to the store and pick up something easy for dinner," Lena announced. "I don't feel like cooking tonight."

"I could cook," Vicki offered immediately. "I've been feeling bad about you doing it all."

Lena eyed her. "I told you I'd let you know when I want you to cook. And don't think I haven't noticed the way you've been cleaning this place. I don't believe it's been this clean since it was built."

Vicki managed a smile. "It's the least I can do."

Lena looked at Dan. "She won't listen to me. She insists on helping out financially, too. I ask you, do I look like I'm poor?"

Dan spread his hands. "I'm not getting into this with you two. Anyway, now you can spend even more than you thought in Denver."

Lena barked a laugh. "Maybe I will."

"As for dinner, I could make chili," Dan said. "You like my chili."

Lena shook her head. "Vicki might not. She's from Texas, don't you know."

At last Vicki was able to let go enough to join in. "Hey!"

"Might be too hot for Krys, though," Lena said, standing. Evidently her mind was made up. "I want something different tonight, so just let me go take care of it. I won't be long."

That left Dan and Vicki sitting at the table by themselves. Vicki had nothing to say, afraid that she would only talk about last night again. Then Dan surprised her back into the present.

"Callie and I wanted children," he remarked.

She looked at him and saw that his face was shadowed. "You didn't get the time?"

"Oh, we had time, we thought. When it finally struck us something might be wrong, we went to the doctor to find out. That's when we learned she had ovarian cancer."

"Oh, Dan. Oh, my…" Words seemed so inadequate. Vicki reached out and he took her hand.

"It still kills me that we didn't know until it was too late. Sometimes I still read all the articles about warnings and signs that need to be checked out, but if Callie ever had any of them, I didn't know it. One day she seemed perfectly healthy, with a whole future ahead of her, and the next day we were facing death. Those kinds of things haunt you. But you know that."

"Yes." But Vicki didn't dare say any more. She waited, giving him some space to talk. After all, they'd agreed they could talk about their late spouses, a subject that generally made others uncomfortable. But apart from that, she really hurt for him.

He averted his face for a few seconds, and she could almost see him absorbing the blow all over again. But then he turned to her again and squeezed her hand. "Krystal's a doll. You're lucky to have her, and I'm lucky I met her."

Vicki answered with a wryness that surprised her, given what she'd been feeling and what they'd been discussing. "She gets her energy from her father. He didn't like holding still. She's not easy to keep up with sometimes."

A smile washed away Dan's haunted expression. "A definite powerhouse."

"Until she runs empty." Vicki hesitated, thinking of the little girl in the next room. She ought to check on her, then told herself she was being overly protective. She'd been trying hard to avoid that, because she didn't want to deprive Krys of a normal childhood, or instill any unnecessary fears in her. The urge was strong today, however, exacerbated by last night.

But she had to consider Dan, too. She didn't want to pop out when he'd been sharing something important with her. It would be rude at the very least, and possibly cruel.

He sighed, rubbing his thumb lightly over the back of her hand. An instant shiver of pleasure passed through her, and a self-protective instinct almost made her snatch her hand back. But she liked his touch. What was so wrong about enjoying it? Besides, he already knew how she felt about a relationship with a cop, how it terrified her. He'd have to be an idiot to have misread that.

He pressed her hand gently, then let go. "How'd we get so maudlin?" he asked. "Oh, yeah. Junior Casson started the show last night. Scares. Reminders. But this time no loss."

Dan's gaze grew intent, earnest. "Just keep reminding yourself of that, Vicki. Krys is all right."

"No thanks to Junior," she said a bit sharply, but then admitted he was right. Maybe she needed to re-examine herself in light of last night's near miss. Apparently cops weren't the only people who could walk out a door and never return.

What a thought! She banished it, not wanting it to pop into her head every time she was away from Krys. "You know," she said suddenly, "it would be so easy to get neurotic."

Dan's eyes widened, then he laughed. "Yeah, it would. I'd really rather not."

"Me, either. I've got enough problems I don't want to pass on to my daughter. Additional ones are not welcome."

His expression softened. "I think you're doing pretty darn good, actually. She seems totally normal to me, in every way."

"Except for the separation anxiety. I hope that passes."

"Too soon to be sure, but she also seems resilient. We must have scared the dickens out of her last night, but she seems fine today."

She certainly did, Vicki thought. Unlike her mother. But maybe that was a blessing of childhood. Last night had scared her, but today everything was happy and upbeat again. Vicki could take some lessons from her. "She seems to have an innate wisdom."

"Or maybe she's far more willing to live in the moment than adults. We're always thinking about tomorrow, or the past, and often overlooking the moment right in front of us."

"Too true," Vicki acknowledged. "Except when we get shocked out of our shoes. That kind of wakes us up." But maybe only briefly. How much time had she spent thinking about last night, instead of just being grateful she still had Krys? Except for a short time when she had felt the blessing, she'd been back-and-forthing about things that had happened and things that might never happen.

"Seems to be human nature after a certain age. God knows how much time I could have spent with Callie that got wasted because I was so busy with anger and grief in anticipation of losing her. Unfortunately, I don't think we can change the way we're built. Nor, I suspect, would the world do so well if nobody learned from the past or looked toward the future."

Vicki gave a quiet laugh. "True. But we could probably spend a little more time actually being here and now."

"Worth a try."

They heard the back door open. Vicki snatched her hand back instantly and Lena entered the kitchen carrying two cloth totes. "Get ready, folks. The butcher will never forget my visit. Big juicy T-bones, specially cut. Dan, you're in charge of grilling. Found some good sweet corn, too, so, Vicki, you can wrap the corn for the grill. You up to it?"

"I thought you didn't want to cook," Vicki said, smiling.

"Did I say *I* was cooking? I seem to be designating everyone else."

Krystal appeared in the doorway, rubbing her eyes. "Can I help, too?"

"See?" said Lena with satisfaction. "Pass me a mint julep. Y'all just got your orders."

Chapter Eight

Watching Lena and her friends depart for Denver turned into a hoot. Six ladies had to load two cars with luggage, decide who was going to sit where and try to decide what hotel to stay in. Vicki suspected some of the lighthearted arguing was for the benefit of their audience, herself and Krys. Finally, Lena jammed her last bag into the back of Rebecca's Toyota.

"It's only three days," Vicki teased. "How are you going to bring anything home with you?"

Rebecca, a slender woman of Lena's age, laughed. "That's what laps and half the backseat are for. Although one year we rented one of those little trailers."

Vicki blinked. "For real? What in the world did you buy?"

"Too much," Lena said drily. "We're older now. We take it to the post office and ship it home."

All the women started laughing and were still laughing when at last they set out.

The Friday afternoon was bright and warm. Vicki took Krystal to the park for a playdate with Peggy, and spent the time talking with Janine Dalrymple and a few other women, one who pushed a stroller back and forth steadily as she watched her two-year-old son play. Her infant slept peacefully the whole time.

In fact, the whole scene was peaceful and nearly perfect. Vicki felt herself uncoiling, in part because she loved the sound of children having a good time.

When the other women learned she had taught kindergarten in Texas, they suddenly bubbled with ideas for her. "You should try to teach at the preschool at Good Shepherd," one said. "I think they need more help."

"Or start your own," said another. "Good Shepherd is too crowded."

"That would be too expensive," Janine said, before Vicki could point it out. "A building, a playground, licensing, hiring other people… That's why the only one we have is at a church."

"I was thinking something else," said the other woman, Daisy. "More like just a couple of hours a day, where kids could get a leg up on reading, the alphabet, numbers. The academic stuff. More personalized attention."

That actually appealed to Vicki. Even though she'd applied for a license here before she'd left Austin, she wasn't sure she was ready to get back into full-time teaching. Her decision to be available to Krys after Hal's death remained with her. It was too soon, especially considering Krys's separation anxiety, for

Vicki to be gone all day. She understood plenty of other mothers weren't blessed with her choices, but since she was, she had chosen what she thought was best.

Which, as with so many things in parenting, might be a two-edged sword.

"I'll think about it," she said as Daisy continued to press her. Vicki returned her attention to Krys, who was now on a swing, talking to another girl as they passed each other in endless arcs. It was also possible that Vicki was making Krys more dependent on her. Crap. Were there no easy, clear answers?

After the park, they walked to town. Krys wanted a hamburger, and since it had been a while since the last junk meal, Vicki decided to give it to her. Besides, she didn't feel like cooking tonight. Her mind seemed preoccupied, though she wasn't exactly sure why.

Dan had been among the missing most of the week, although he had a reason for it. They were approaching championship season in baseball, which seemed a little ludicrous to her. Apparently, the Little League needed some extra umpires, so he was there every evening he could be, helping out. At least he'd dropped by on his way home, staying for a brief chat with her and Krys.

Vicki missed him, and was surprised that Krys hadn't been carrying on about it. She always greeted him with huge excitement, but didn't seem to have a problem with him being needed elsewhere. Once, Krys had said that she wanted to go to a baseball game, and Vicki had promised they'd go next week.

She was just entering the courthouse square, right before the turn to Maude's, when she saw Dan come out of the sheriff's office. Once again, for the first time since the fair, she saw him in full uniform. Her heart jolted and she would have frozen in place if Krys hadn't spied him and cried his name. *It's not the same,* Vicki told herself. Hal's uniform had been dark blue. This uniform was khaki. Different.

Oh, hell, it wasn't different at all. The badge, the belt with the gun, the white plastic restraints hanging like loose loops on his hip…no, it wasn't different.

Dan heard Krys call his name. He smiled and waved, and trotted toward them, making an exaggerated effort to look in every direction before crossing the street. In spite of herself, Vicki had to laugh.

"Two of my favorite ladies," he said warmly when he reached them. "How's my pumpkin?" he asked as he lifted Krys for a hug.

"Super," Krys answered, her new favorite word. "I'm getting a hamburger."

"Oh, that sounds yummy. No pickles, right?"

"Nope. Mommy always gets pickles." Krys made an exaggerated face.

"So she's a sourpuss?"

That sent Krys into a gale of laughter as Dan set her down. He smiled at Vicki. "How's Mom doing?"

"I'm just fine," she answered. "Are you off on an important mission?"

"Actually, I was about to go in search of food. We had a busy day, and I haven't eaten since breakfast. I was thinking about calling you and asking if you wanted me to bring dinner home with me, but you beat me. Mind some company?"

"Of course not."

Krys clung to both their hands as they walked, crossing one more street, then turning toward the City Diner.

"What was so busy?" Vicki asked.

"Youthful miscreants. Too much time on their hands this summer, school's about to start again, and I guess they figured this was their last chance to misbehave. Heck, I don't know. The Little League championships have some people wound up, too, and a lot of folks have come to town for the weekend games."

"For real?" It amazed her.

"Hey, for some it's important. Important enough to overimbibe, to forget that the sun is supposed to pass the yardarm first...you get the idea. Speeders, vandals and inebriates, and some fisticuffs. You could almost swear something gets into the water from time to time."

She noted the way he tried to phrase it so Krys couldn't follow, and Vicki expected a raft of questions from her daughter. But Krys seemed to be more interested in getting to the diner.

"Summer's almost over," Dan said as they approached the restaurant. "The last hurrah. Until cabin fever sets in sometime this winter, anyway."

Coming from Texas, Vicki couldn't imagine summer being over already. "I'd still be thinking fall was a bit down the road in Austin."

"I imagine so," he said as he opened the door. "We'll probably see our first snow flurry here while you Texans are just starting autumn. Or not." He looked down at Krystal. "Ever been sledding?"

She shook her head.

"We will definitely have to take care of that."

She imagined sitting behind Dan on a sled, her legs and arms wrapped around him, and decided they would definitely have to try sledding. A small smile danced across her face.

The place was fairly crowded, but Dan managed to get them a table near the window. Or maybe Maude, the owner, did. She kind of pushed them toward it.

"She's sweet on you," Vicki couldn't resist murmuring to Dan, although she suspected she might be projecting her own feelings. Was she getting sweet on him? Instead of being terrified by the thought, she actually tucked it away and savored it.

"Hey, I'm a sweet guy." He winked humorously.

Their dinners were served, and Vicki talked about the school idea the women had suggested, because it seemed utterly safe. Dan listened, nodding, and Krystal appeared more involved with her giant hamburger.

"I agree setting up a preschool would be an awfully expensive venture," he said. "But a tutoring kind of program for an hour or two a day? I bet a lot of people would be interested. The church preschool *is* overloaded. They're trying to raise funds right now to expand, because they've reached their code limits."

"Well, it's just an idea, and that's all it's going to be, at least for a while."

He smiled. "Try taking some deep breaths and getting your feet under you first."

He was right about that. She felt far from settled yet, and while she was beginning to make some community ties herself, she still had to put Krystal first. The women at the park had been fun and encouraging, very welcoming, but Vicki was still waiting to feel as if she and her daughter had truly landed. Something a little like jet lag struck her every so often, a sense of unreality. She guessed her big move wasn't yet complete, at least emotionally.

Still, it was kind of nice to play around with the tutoring idea. Her days were full enough, with Krystal, and helping Lena take care of the house, and while Vicki hadn't thought about it much in the past year, she was beginning to feel some needs of her own, such as wanting to accomplish something. Teaching kindergarten had often given her the sense that she was doing something important that extended out beyond her immediate family. Apparently, that need hadn't entirely gone away. Little by little it was reawakening, and tutoring seemed like a gentle way to reintroduce Krys to the idea that her mom worked.

A good example for the child, a necessity for herself, and something that probably would wait until Krystal started school next year. Vicki's whole purpose in leaving her job last time had been to make sure Krystal got over the hump of losing her father, that she knew at least one of her parents was always there.

Maybe that wouldn't be so important a few months down the road, but so soon after their move, Vicki still worried. Krys seemed to be transplanting well and thriving, but there were still those moments that worried her.

When it came to true stability for Krys, Vicki figured she was it.

After their early supper, the two of them walked back to the house carrying a bag of leftovers. Dan returned to the sheriff's office, mentioning he'd probably be home soon.

"Come see us," Krys invited.

Dan looked at Vicki, who smiled and nodded. It no longer totally terrified her that she wanted to see this man often. Just as long as she kept things in safe limits, that was.

"You got it, pumpkin. I'll be there soon."

It struck Vicki as they were walking home that it might not be good for Dan to make such promises. She'd already seen that he could get called in on a moment's notice. What's more, a department with only about twenty-five deputies probably needed a lot of officers to step up if something happened, or if one got sick. Filling in the gaps was probably a large part of Dan's job.

And then there was the other problem: the possibility that he might not come home at all. She felt only marginally better since he'd told her that they hadn't lost a deputy in a couple decades. It could still happen.

But for the first time, she wondered if her fear might be irrational. Yes, being a cop could be dangerous, but when she looked back over her years with Hal, the only death had been his. And he hadn't even been on duty.

Her throat tightened and she swallowed hard. Hal going to the store to get milk. Sometimes she got so angry, wondering if he wouldn't have been killed if he hadn't tried to be the good cop. He hadn't even been on duty. Maybe interfering in the robbery had cost him his life. But on duty or off duty, he'd been a cop. He could have just as easily walked into that mess wearing his uniform.

She tried to tell herself it could have happened to anyone in the store that night, but she didn't quite believe it. Hal had put it all out there, trying to protect the store manager and other patrons. It was too late to second-guess his decisions, to wonder whether, if he hadn't challenged the perp, the guy might have walked out with his miserable twenty bucks. A man's life for twenty dollars. It still appalled her.

"Mommy?"

Yanked back into the present, Vicki glanced down. "Yes?"

"Will Dan really come?"

There it was again, tightening Vicki's throat once more. Maybe she should speak to Dan about saying things with much less certainty. "He said he would. But he has to work, too, so we can't be sure."

"I know."

There was something dark in the girl's tone, and it frightened Vicki. What demon was she dealing with now?

Vicki squatted on the sidewalk and Krys automatically turned to look at her. "Krys, are you worried Dan won't come?"

She tilted her head before answering. "No," she said finally. "He said he would."

"Then you're worried about him being late?" God, Vicki hoped that was all it was.

"Yup. Can we go home and play a game?"

"Of course." They resumed walking, but Vicki's heart felt like lead. Late? Oh, she didn't think that was it at all, especially since Dan hadn't promised a time. Maybe seeing him in uniform had stirred some reaction in Krys, one she wasn't even aware of.

Was Vicki making a mistake, allowing this friendship? But how could she stop it now? Her daughter wasn't the only one who'd become dependent on Dan.

Dan didn't keep Krystal waiting for long. An hour later, dressed in jeans and a black sweatshirt, he popped through the door, looking guilty. In his hand he carried a bag.

Krystal greeted him joyfully, and Dan swung her up into his arms. They all moved into the living room and sat on the sofa. Dan eyed Vicki. "Get annoyed with me if you want."

"About what?"

"I heard what you said about the tide of gifts, but I brought one, anyway."

Vicki, inexplicably relieved that he had shown up and put Krys's concerns to rest, merely laughed. "What did you do?"

"Don't hate me forever." He reached for the bag and pulled out a stuffed gray-and-white wolf, just a small one, but suitable for carrying around. He handed it to Krys. "Your very first wolf."

She squealed in pleasure and said thank-you before crawling into Dan's lap, holding her new treasure.

"It's beautiful," Vicki said, admiring the wolf, and happy with Krys's reaction. Apparently, whatever had troubled her was gone now. Vicki didn't want to think about that.

"Not easy to find," Dan remarked. "Ranchers don't care for the wolves at all, and we've got a pack up on Thunder Mountain. It's not the kind of thing most people around here would want to buy."

Vicki had read about the problems, the concern on the part of ranchers that wolves presented a threat to livestock. She got it, but didn't say any more about it. She was the newbie here, and reading up on something didn't make her an expert.

"I like wolfs," Krys said.

"Wolves," Vicki corrected gently. "I know, it seems dumb, but that's the way it is."

Krys giggled and admired her new toy while leaning against Dan's chest. "This is a wolfie," she announced.

"Fair enough," Vicki agreed. She glanced at Dan and saw him looking down at Krys with a slightly wistful smile. Clearly, he was enjoying having her on his lap, and enjoyed her pleasure in the wolf, but Vicki could only imagine what other thoughts must be running through his head. Perhaps he was thinking about the daughter he might have had.

Between the two of them, she guessed she was by far the luckier.

He suggested they play a game, and Krys ran to get one. When she came back downstairs, she was carrying the children's version of Scrabble. Vicki felt a little surprised. Krys hadn't shown much interest in it lately.

"Wow, that's heavy," Dan said. "I'm not the world's best speller. Are you sure you want to play with me?"

"Mommy will fix it if you're wrong."

With that assurance they adjourned to the dining room. With a new player in the mix, Krys seemed to have regained her liking of the game, and often laughed delightedly when Dan made an obvious mistake and Vicki fixed it. She suspected most of those mistakes were on purpose, but Krys had a lot of fun. In fact, they all did.

But eventually Krys tired and needed to go to bed. Dan remained downstairs while mother and daughter followed the nightly ritual. At least Krys didn't want to hear Bartholomew Cubbins again, but instead chose a very elementary Dr. Seuss book she could mostly read herself.

Afterward, Vicki went back downstairs. Dan had

made coffee and waited in the kitchen, offering her a cup as soon as she appeared.

All of a sudden, she felt nervous. Lena was gone, Krys was already sleeping and Vicki was utterly alone with a man she found incredibly attractive. A man who had kissed her not once but twice, which kind of indicated he was interested.

Slowly, she sat at the table and wrapped her hands around her mug.

"What's wrong?" Dan asked, studying her. "Krystal?"

She shook her head quickly. "She's fine. Sound asleep already. I wish I could drift off as fast as she does."

He smiled. "Clear conscience."

A quiet laugh escaped Vicki. "Maybe so." But she didn't feel like laughing, not really. Part of her wanted to take advantage of this rare privacy, and part of her was terrified of it.

Words burst out of her. "I'm getting awfully tired of being a responsible adult."

His smile widened a shade. "I can certainly believe it. You need to make some room for yourself, Vicki. I understand how many obligations you have, and I'm not suggesting you run off for a wild weekend and leave Krys behind. But you need to find something to do just for your own enjoyment."

She was sure he was right. The problem was the only thing she wanted to enjoy right now was being in a man's arms again, the world banished by the wonder of lovemaking. Worse, the only arms she wanted around her were Dan's.

"Maybe I should go," he said presently. "You're looking skittish, and I get the feeling I'm the problem."

"Reading minds again?" she asked, even though he was exactly right.

"Reading faces," he said. He pushed his mug aside and reached for both her hands, holding them gently. "We both know what's going on here. We're attracted. You don't want it. In fairness, I'm having a few qualms myself. There's been nobody since Callie, and I feel a little guilty about how much I want you. Just a bit guilty. Well, if I can feel guilt after five years, it's got to be worse for you."

Talk about blunt. Vicki's cheeks flamed, and she wanted desperately to break their gaze, but she couldn't. Those warm gray eyes held her as surely as a spell. "It's not just that," she said, astonished at the way her voice had thickened. Her heart began a steady throbbing, whether from fear or anticipation, she couldn't have guessed. Once again heavy heat pooled between her thighs.

"Well, I'm sure it doesn't help that I'm a cop." He sighed, released her hands and went to dump his coffee in the sink and rinse his cup. He paused by her chair, touching her shoulder briefly. "I'll see you tomorrow. I've got two games in the afternoon, but otherwise... we'll see."

Then he was walking to the front door. A crazy desperation filled her. Before her mind and fears could take charge, she jumped up, answering a deeper need that refused to be denied.

"Dan!" She reached the foyer. "Don't go."

He hesitated with his hand on the doorknob, looking back at her. "Vicki, I'd never forgive myself if I hurt you."

"I'm… You…" She couldn't find the words. "Oh, for Pete's sake, just stay, unless you want to go." Heading into the living room, she plopped down on the couch and folded her arms.

What the hell was she doing? Better yet, what had gotten into her? She couldn't believe the weird way she was acting. Fearful, irritable and hungry all rolled up in one. What did she expect from the man? Clearly, she had problems, and he was simply trying not to make them worse.

Although really, he should have thought of all that before he'd kissed her and held her the other night. Pandora's box was now wide-open, and she couldn't decide which of the world's troubles were emerging from it. If troubles they were.

She heard Dan's step. He came into the living room and sat right beside her on the couch. Their shoulders brushed, but he didn't try to embrace her.

"Talk to me if you can," he suggested.

"I'm confused!" That at least was true.

"I gathered that." He sighed. "You know, some things ought to be as easy as rolling off a log. Too bad there seem to be brambles everywhere."

A great description. She relaxed a hair, but didn't shift position. Her folded arms said she was closed off, and she knew it. But she didn't feel any need to open up. Not yet. Not when a whirlwind seemed to have taken possession of her senses.

Minutes ticked by while she sorted through her personal morass and tried to pick out what was really important. Krystal, of course, but even Vicki knew she couldn't continue to make her daughter the center of her life indefinitely. Krys was growing up. In a few years the last person she was going to want to hang with all the time was her mother. She'd make friends, find activities, expand her horizons.

So Vicki needed to do some fixing of her own. Life would move on, and she'd come here to make it happen. If anything was holding her back, it was her.

"Dan?"

"Yeah?"

"I can't figure it out."

"What, exactly?"

"Me. The more I try to figure things out, the messier they get. I swore I'd never get involved with a cop again. Well, look at me now."

"We're just friends."

At that she unfolded her arms and twisted to face him. "That makes it better how? You think I'd care any less if you didn't come home tomorrow night?"

"Whoa." His eyes widened a bit. "What are you saying?"

"Obviously, I care about you. You've become a good friend. Krys cares about you. It's not like it wouldn't be a blip on the emotional radar if you disappeared."

He frowned. "But I don't have to make it worse."

"Worse is a matter of degree, and you don't have to do anything. This isn't about anything you've done. It's about me and my crazy, mixed-up feelings. Sure, I get it. Anyone could walk out that door and never come back. My God, it was only a week ago that I nearly lost Krys."

He nodded, studying her intently, but evidently deciding to let her ramble on without interruption.

That was the problem, though—she was rambling around in her own confusion. He couldn't sort it out for her, and she was doing a lousy job of it herself.

"I want you," she admitted finally. It was possibly the one thing she was sure about, apart from her daughter. Blunt, bold, concealing nothing of her inner turmoil, but useless in sorting herself out. Only one thing she could figure out, that she wanted this man?

"But?"

"I don't know. I'm afraid. I told you that. Not of you, but of your damn job. Maybe that's unreasonable. You tried to tell me that, and you're probably right, but how do you argue with feelings?"

"You can't," he agreed. His face grew shadowed, but only for an instant. Once again, he listened attentively.

"Like the other night, when you risked your life to save Krystal. That's the kind of man you are. It was the kind of man Hal was. He didn't have to get involved in that store robbery. He was off duty. He could have ducked with everyone else and called 911. Instead, he chose to confront the robber. He wasn't even wearing his vest. Why would he be? He went to the store for milk. For *milk*!"

Dan nodded, and at last looped his arm loosely around her shoulder.

"But I get it intellectually," she ranted on. "Oh, yes, I get it. The store manager could have been shot. An ordinary customer could have died. Hal's being a cop didn't necessarily have anything to do with the outcome. Ordinary people get killed every day doing ordinary things. But tell that to my heart."

"You're angry with him."

"Yes, I am! I'm furious! He never gave one thought to his daughter when he acted."

"Or to you," Dan said quietly.

"Or to me." She lost her steam, and her voice became small. "Nobody else entered his head. Just like nothing entered your head when you saw Krystal in danger. Heroes. God deliver me."

"Damn, woman," Dan said, sounding bemused and a bit startled. "I'd have done what anyone would. You were trying to get there yourself."

"But I'm her *mother*. It's programmed into me. What's programmed into you, Dan Casey?"

"The same thing that's programmed into you," he said quietly. "Tell me you wouldn't have tried to save any child, even one you didn't know. Because if you do, I won't believe you. That's not heroic. It's human."

Even in her distressed state, Vicki had to admit he was making sense. Would she have chased *any* child? Probably. But that didn't resolve the entire issue. She didn't make traffic stops, or report to domestic disturbances, two of the most dangerous things any cop could do.

On the other hand, how many Austin police officers had died during the time she had known Hal? Only him. And before that? Even Hal had dismissed it, much as Dan did. She couldn't remember how long it had been, according to Hal, but it had been a while. Maybe she'd exaggerated the dangers.

But she had faced them up close and personal. No arguing with that.

Dan's arm tightened around her shoulders. "You can't sort it all out at once," he said finally. "It'll come with time."

"You'd have the experience to know," she admitted. She turned her head and let it rest against his shoulder. "What I'm doing makes about as much sense as you never finding another woman to love because something bad might happen."

"Well, I haven't exactly been looking." Not until this blue-eyed beauty had popped her head out a door, looking tired, dusty and very much alone. "But I'm not a kid anymore. When the time is right, the person is right…" He shrugged. She felt the movement beneath her ear.

"It used to be so easy," she murmured.

"It's still easy. It just hurts more. But there's only one thing to do, and we've both been doing it—taking one step at a time. Day in and day out. Just take the next step. You took a huge one coming here. So I guess, much as it may terrify you, that you still have some hope."

"Hope?"

"For a better future." He tightened his arm around her, turning it into a hug. "You haven't given up, Vicki. I don't think it's in you. I mean, you could have stayed in the cocoon in Austin, surrounded by people you know and care about. It would have been easy. Instead, you decided you needed to build a different future. That requires hope."

"Or desperation," she said with something between amusement and bitterness. Everything inside her seemed to have been tossed into a blender somehow. She'd focused on two things for a year: grief and Krystal. Moving here had shifted her focus in some essential way. She no longer had just two major things to deal with. Now she had longings she wasn't prepared for, and a friend named Dan who drew her as strongly as anything in her life ever had.

The right man with the wrong job. Damn! She wondered if she might be crazy, making the same mistake over again when she ought to have learned.

But had she learned the right lesson or the wrong lesson? Danged if she knew.

"Love hurts sometimes," Dan said. "We both know that. But I wouldn't have missed a single moment with Callie to have avoided the pain. Maybe you're not ready to feel that way yet, but I hope you get there."

Maybe that's why everything inside Vicki felt all mixed up. Maybe she *was* transitioning, changing. She believed she had needed to, believed it enough that she had uprooted her daughter and moved far away from all the reminders.

Well, except for a certain man who wore a uniform that reminded her. That probably wasn't fair to either herself or Dan, to categorize him by a badge. But the fear still lingered, a miasma she couldn't quite blow away.

"Nothing has to be settled right now," he reminded her. "Big changes require lots of time. I just want you to know something."

She tipped her head to see his face. "Yes?"

"I want you, too. I can't set eyes on you without getting hot and heavy. So if you ever decide to risk it…"

She caught her breath. She knew what he was doing. She'd exposed herself to him, and now he was giving her the same in return, so she wouldn't feel stupid and vulnerable. But apart from that, she realized how much she liked hearing him say it. Warmth drizzled through her again, trying to drive out all the doubts, creating an ache inside her that was huge. *Wanting* barely scratched the surface of the needs he awoke in her.

This ought to be between the two of them, but she doubted it would be that simple. There was Krystal to consider, and the likelihood she would come to care even more deeply for Dan.

That still frightened Vicki. If they moved into a romantic relationship and it didn't work, how could they carry on as friends if they broke up? How would that affect Krystal? Her daughter's attachment to Dan was already painfully clear. To risk anything that would sever that connection…

Vicki leaned forward, out of Dan's embrace, and put her face in her hands. Her body was racked with unanswered needs and longings, so hungry for this man it almost hurt. Every cell seemed to have wakened to possibilities, to the anticipation of pleasure, and except for one little girl, she'd probably dive in headfirst without another thought.

She might be acting unreasonably about the cop thing, or maybe not, but her fears for Krys were well-founded.

Finally, Vicki lifted her head. "Dan, whatever happens, you'd still be friends with Krys?"

"I'm surprised you need to ask. That girl has wormed into my heart in a very special way. It'd take a restraining order to stop me from being her friend." He paused. "I'll still be friends with you, too, Vicki. No matter what. It *is* possible."

"As long as I don't turn into a raging shrew."

He sounded truly curious. "You? Do you ever do that?"

"I never have, but there's always a first time."

He laughed. "I'll believe it when I see it."

She envied how comfortable he seemed with all this. He was an accepting man, she realized. Rarely if ever criticizing, seeming to take people as they came. With the possible exception of Junior Casson, but that was different.

"Were you always like this?" she asked.

"Like what?"

"So calm and accepting. So relaxed. I've just put you through the weirdest conversation, and you seem comfortable. Wouldn't most guys be heading for the hills by now?"

"I can't speak for most guys. I have no desire to head for the hills. And if I'm accepting, maybe it's because I've had to learn to accept myself since Callie became sick. But remember how I suggested that you need something in life just for yourself, Vicki. I'm not saying it's me, but you need something you can look forward to. You handle responsibility well, but doesn't there have to be something else?"

"Do you get that from your coaching and baseball?"

"Some of it, yes. It started as a way to keep busy, but now I love it. I look forward to the practices and games. This winter it'll be basketball."

"So it's not exactly selfish. You're helping others at the same time."

He gave a quiet laugh. "It's mostly selfish. I enjoy it too much to think of it any other way. Just like I enjoy an occasional poker game, going to the movies, hanging out at Mahoney's with a few friends and visiting with the three of you."

She was touched that he included them in his list of things he enjoyed. Especially since she hadn't always been fun or easy to deal with. "When Krys gets into kindergarten next year—"

He stopped her, touching her lips lightly with a finger. "No putting it off for a year. Maybe it would be good for Krys to know you enjoy something besides being a mommy. That you get some me time." He paused. "Not my place to say, I guess."

"Oh, it's your place. Why not? You've practically become family for her and me. I respect your judgment, anyway."

"But I've never been a parent." He arched a brow. "I've found that parents don't like advice from people who've never done the job."

She had to laugh, however weak it sounded. "They don't like it from teachers, either."

"Pity. There's a world of wisdom available from some folks."

Vicki leaned back and his arm surrounded her again, making her feel good, and this time it helped her relax a bit. Oh, her hunger for him was still present, but he offered something else, something amazingly close to solace.

Whatever came, she no longer doubted that she had found a great friend in Dan Casey.

Eventually, conversation moved to lighter subjects, matters that didn't leave her drained from struggling with them. Remembering Hal's hyperkinetic nature, she recalled how she had loved the excitement he always seemed to bring with him. Now, however, she was discovering a new experience, the experience of being able to enjoy just relaxing with someone. It was peaceful, and not at all boring. Comfortable and friendly.

"Are you going to be all right alone here tonight?"

Dan asked. "I know you're used to having your own place. I just wondered if this being a different house might make you feel differently. So far Lena has always been here at night."

Vicki hadn't even considered it. It hadn't been looming in front of her like some daunting task. Her instinct was to say she'd be fine, but then she wondered. It *was* a different house, much bigger than any she had lived in before. Getting used to being alone after Hal's death had given her some difficult moments, even though he'd worked plenty of night shifts. Things seemed different in the dark, and even familiar noises could take on a whole new quality. She wasn't familiar with this house yet, and without Lena nearby, or Krys filling the place with her energy and chatter, Vicki wondered if it was going to feel like an echoing cavern.

"Why did you have to mention that?" she asked. "I wasn't even thinking about it."

"Sorry." But then he laughed. "I wasn't trying to scare you. It's just that I need my bed soon. I have an early half day tomorrow, followed by two games. So... I'd rather you think about it before you're all alone here and pacing the floor because something disturbs you. I can camp on this couch easily enough."

"You wouldn't sleep well," she argued, even though the idea appealed to her.

"Wanna bet? I go out like a light."

"I don't know, Dan. I appreciate the offer, but I need to get used to this sooner or later."

"True." He stood. "Then I'll just head on home. But if anything makes you nervous, call me. I sleep with the phone beside my bed. For obvious reasons."

She looked at him standing there, and felt desire

drowning her again. How could any man make jeans and a black sweatshirt look so good? It's not as if he'd dressed to show off, but even a sweatshirt couldn't conceal powerful shoulders, and the jeans accentuated his narrow, hard hips. She longed to run her hands up under that shirt and learn the feel of his skin, and if his muscles would ripple at her touch. Such long legs, too. She bet he'd look great in shorts. Or naked.

He sighed. "If you keep looking at me like that I *will* be spending the night here."

Her heart leaped, then crashed immediately. He turned for the door. "Conversation to be continued at a later date, when you're *really* ready. See you tomorrow."

He'd almost reached the door when she couldn't stand it. Forgetting everything else, she jumped up. "Dan!"

He turned, saw her hurrying toward him. He opened his mouth to ask a question, then apparently saw the answer on her face.

"Vicki…" He sounded almost cautionary, but she kept hurrying toward him and at last his arms closed around her, his mouth covered hers and everything inside her washed away in an explosion of passion. One thing for herself? This was it. She cast all thought of risks and ramifications aside, needing this more than she had needed anything in a very long time. The hunger had been dancing around the edge of her awareness almost from the start. Now it consumed her, a fire gone wild. She ached. She yearned. Every cell in her awoke, crying for his touches, demanding satisfaction.

His tongue plunged into her mouth, tasting her with almost as much desperation as a starving man tasted food. When at last he tore his mouth away, they were both dragging in air as if there wasn't enough of it in the universe.

"Be sure," he said hoarsely. "Just be sure."

Her voice emerged in a rusty-sounding whisper. "I am if you are."

He seemed to have no doubts at all. Astonishing her, he swept her up in his arms. "Krystal," he said thickly.

Vicki hadn't thought of that, and for one instant it almost killed her desire. What if her daughter heard them, or came in? "My room is down the hall." In this old house, sounds didn't carry room to room if the doors were closed.

That seemed to settle it for him. He carried her up the wide staircase, a remnant of better times, while she looped an arm around his shoulders and clung. She could feel the power of the muscles that carried her, and a renewed thrill raced through her. With each step, the throbbing ache within her deepened.

Passion ruled her now, and she didn't have even a flicker of doubt, or a concern that she might be making a big mistake. She needed what Dan was offering, and he seemed to want it, too. The rest could wait.

As he set her on her feet beside the bed, and kissed her again, she felt all the flutters, nervousness and excitement of a first time. Even though she'd been married four years and had borne a child, right then she felt sixteen and caught in the enchantment of an utterly new experience, one she wanted with breathless anticipation.

After releasing her mouth so that they could both breathe again, Dan trailed kisses along her jaw. His breath, warm and a bit ragged, entered her ear, causing her to shiver with delight.

"You nervous?" he asked.

"Plenty."

"Me, too."

His admission ignited a spark in her. She tipped her head almost coquettishly for the first time in forever, and gave him a sidelong glance. "Are we going to hold a meeting or just jump each other's bones?"

"I forgot the roses and chocolate," he said, laughter in his voice. "So jump it is."

All of a sudden Vicki realized that she felt free, truly free, for the first time in forever. Reaching out, she began to tug his sweatshirt up with all the eagerness of a kid opening a present. This was *her* present. A special hour or two just for her. The sweatshirt went flying at last, and she stared at his chest in the moonlight that bathed the room. Her heart hammered, her blood pounded until it was loud in her ears. Every cell seemed suspended in a moment of almost painful anticipation.

"Who made you so beautiful?" she breathed, running her hands over his pecs, her palms finding the nubs of his small nipples. So absorbed was she in admiring him, in feeling his warm skin and the way his muscles moved and quivered beneath her touch, that she hardly noticed when her own T-shirt and bra vanished into some dark corner in the room.

"You're exquisite," he said hoarsely. "Perfect." His hands cupped her breasts, at first just holding them. But then his thumbs began to torture her nipples, each brush and gentle pinch sending ribbons of fresh fire through her.

She ached, oh, how she ached, and her entire body screamed for him to enter her, now, now…now. Demands rose in her, speechless but no less powerful. There was only one answer to the pounding hunger in her, and it was Dan deep inside her. She became an aching emptiness that only he could fill.

He took her mouth in another kiss, plunging his tongue into her as he himself would, soon. She began to move in rhythm with his strokes, even as he played with her nipples, until she was clinging to his shoulders and arching backward, trying to bring her hips closer to his.

The room spun. Almost as soon as she felt her back hit the bed, her shoes and jeans vanished. She lay naked in the moonlight and he towered over her, drinking her in, the very touch of his gaze fueling her passion as surely as the touch of his hands and mouth.

He stripped quickly, and soon hovered over her on the bed. Her legs parted, her need to welcome him so strong that she didn't want to waste any more time.

He knelt until he had rolled a condom onto his full erection, then seemed almost to hesitate. She couldn't stand it another second. Half rising, she grabbed his shoulders and pulled him down on her. Moments later he slipped inside her and she let out a groan of sheer delight.

At last!

The passion that drove them was impatient. It swept them up and away so swiftly that in no time at all, Vicki felt herself teetering on the painful yet glorious brink of completion. Part of her wanted to hover there forever, but with one more stroke he pushed her over, and an instant later she felt the shudder of completion take him.

A million fireworks exploded inside her. The world vanished. All that remained was the man who held her.

Chapter Nine

Dan didn't want to move. He didn't care if he never moved again. He could have died a happy man wrapped in Vicki's delightful body.

But as always, awareness returned. He had to withdraw, get to the bathroom, take care of necessary matters. He hated reality for a few seconds.

He stirred and kissed her gently. "Be right back."

He pulled on his jeans and sweatshirt in case Krys came out of her room, then headed to the hall bath. He washed quickly, then just as quickly returned to the bedroom. Vicki still lay naked and uncovered, silvered by moonlight, looking like a faerie. But she, too, had returned to earth. She lifted a foot and wagged it at him.

"Socks. We forgot about socks." Then she giggled. The sound made him smile, and filled him with pleasure. So far, so good. He sat on the edge of the bed, sprinkling kisses on her face, then grasping her hand.

Her expression changed. "Are you bailing?"

"Absolutely not. I'm admiring you. I liked that big Cheshire grin on your face, so put it back."

Another giggle escaped her. "Wow," she said quietly, and rolled on her side, wrapping one arm around his hips.

"Wow," he agreed. He supposed he ought to say something about how he'd be slower next time, that he didn't usually make love with all the finesse of a horse racing back to the barn. But then he skipped it. If she allowed them another time together, he'd have a chance to show her.

She squirmed some more until her cheek rested on his denim-covered thigh. He couldn't resist stroking her silky shoulder. "Dan."

"Yeah?"

"Just saying your name. I like it. I like everything about you."

He didn't mention the badge that was causing her so much concern. He didn't want to disrupt the beauty that suffused the room, filled both of them. That showered its blessings in the argent moonlight.

He squeezed her shoulder. "Can I get you anything? Food, beverage?"

She sighed and sat up with clear reluctance. "You said you needed sleep tonight."

"Believe me, I can go on short sleep for one night. Trying to throw me out?"

"Not hardly." She pressed her face to his shoulder and inhaled his wonderful scent. "Unfortunately, the world doesn't go on vacation. I need to put something on. What if Krys comes looking for me? She's still doing that some nights."

Reluctantly, Dan stood, acknowledging the justice of her concern. They could explain this a whole bunch of ways to her daughter. He was fully dressed, her mom could hide under sheets... But why run the risk? The last thing he ever wanted to do was create any kind of problem for that little girl. Kids, he'd noticed, seemed to have built-in lie detectors, and evasions rarely satisfied them.

Vicki rose and pulled on her clothes again. He watched with enjoyment, then redirected his own attention long enough to put on his shoes. They went downstairs holding hands, and into the kitchen to make fresh coffee. If coffee ever started keeping him up at night, he didn't know what he'd do. Staff of life and all that.

Vicki pulled out some banana bread and cut a few thick slabs. "I hope it's not stale," she said. "I made it a couple of days ago."

He pronounced it perfect and he meant it. "It's not too sweet."

"That's because I let the bananas do all the sweetening. Kids get enough sugar without me adding to it."

He and Callie had often done this, sitting together at their kitchen table for a late-night snack. His mind traveled back over the years, and he could almost hear her voice again, reminding him of the promise she'd extracted from him.

"Callie made me promise something."

Dan felt Vicki's gaze on him, and wondered if he had just achieved the world's highest score for bad timing. He had made love to this woman only a short time ago, and now he was talking about Callie? He ought to quit right now before he really messed things up.

But Vicki's hand covered his. "What did she make you promise?"

"That I wouldn't turn into a lonely, crusty old widower. She said I wasn't built to be crusty."

"I'd agree with her," Vicki answered softly.

"Anyway, she was pretty definite about it. She said we'd had our time together, that we were damn lucky to have had it, and she made me promise to start living again."

"She was a very loving woman."

"Yes. She was." He sighed, passed his hand over his eyes. Tears, long gone, didn't return now. He guessed he'd made some peace at last. "I was listening to her, and I promised, but at the time I was thinking if this is life, I don't want much more of it."

"Oh, Dan…"

But he could hear that Vicki understood perfectly what he meant. Of course she would. Her loss had come more swiftly, but the piper got paid all the same. Mountains of grief, guilt and anger.

"Anyway, I thought of that because Callie and I used to do this—sit up late at the kitchen table and have coffee with something sweet."

Vicki hesitated, then asked, "Would you prefer to sit in the other room?"

"No." He shook his head a bit. "No, I was just realizing… I guess I've made peace. It's okay. It's very much okay."

He looked at her then, wondering how she'd take that. She hadn't had nearly as much time as he. Of course, peace came in its own good time. No calendar dictated it.

"I think," she said after a few minutes, "that I had it easier than you. No lingering, painful illness. Just a swift end."

"But unexpected," he reminded her. "That had to be hard."

"Of course. But I had Krystal. That made me lucky. When I least wanted to carry on, I had to. Most of the time when I just wanted to go wallow, I couldn't. And I was rarely alone because of her. I had a focus beyond Hal's loss. And I had a piece of him. She looks a little like him. Well, you saw his photo up in her room, didn't you? There was a time when I couldn't look at her without seeing his face. Now I mostly see Krys, and I guess that's a good thing."

"Probably."

"She can't become a monument to her father. Not in my mind most of all. So did Callie have any directions about how you were to live the rest of your life?"

That surprised a laugh from him and returned comfort to the room. "Actually, no. She did tell me once that she'd haunt me mercilessly if I didn't get on with life."

"Has she been around?"

"Sometimes I feel as if she's close." He shrugged one shoulder. "Maybe I imagine it."

"I feel Hal, too. I'm not so sure it's imagination." Their fingers twined, and they shared a moment of deep understanding. "It's like a whisper of feeling. A sense. Sometimes it's almost so strong I'm convinced that if I just had ears to hear or eyes to see, he'd be right there. I know how that sounds, like wishful thinking, but it feels so real. Then it's gone, like it never happened." She looked down at their clasped hands. "It doesn't happen so often anymore."

"For me, either."

They shared another look of understanding.

"I guess," Vicki said, "that I'm moving on. It sounds awful, but it's necessary. Callie was right about that. That's why I moved up here. Time to get on with the rest of it, whatever it is. I'd like you to stay tonight, Dan. But you need some sleep. I get it. So…"

Before she could finish, they heard Krystal coming downstairs. Vicki gave Dan a wry look before withdrawing her hand. "What did I tell you?"

"I think kids have radar."

"It's entirely possible."

Clad in her pink, ruffled nightgown with pink bunny slippers on her feet, Krys stumbled sleepily into the kitchen.

"Something wrong, honey?"

"Hungry."

Vicki widened her eyes comically. "Really? After that big burger?"

Krys smiled sleepily. "I didn't eat it all," she reminded her mother. Then, as naturally as if she'd been doing it forever, she held out her arms to Dan. He swung her up into his lap so she faced the table.

"I see some banana bread," he said. "Want some?"

"Yummy," Krys answered. Her head drooped against his shoulder.

Vicki jumped up and went to get another slice. She put the plate and a fork in front of her daughter.

"Dan?" Krys said.

"Yes, pumpkin?"

"Don't go away tonight."

The words jolted him. She'd said them once before to him, but now he wondered how often Vicki had been hearing them. Their eyes locked over her daughter's head. He could see the concern on Vicki's face, but he wasn't at all sure how to handle this.

Vicki was gnawing her lower lip. He waited for her guidance on how she wanted to proceed. She surprised him, because this time she addressed the question directly.

"Why don't you want Dan to go home, Krys? It's just next door and we'll see him tomorrow."

"I like Dan," she answered simply. Krys seemed more awake, and she sat up, reaching for her pumpkin bread.

"We all like Dan," Vicki agreed. "But you're going back to bed soon, and he needs to go home to sleep."

"He can sleep here," she stated promptly, then filled her mouth with pumpkin bread.

"How come?" Vicki asked. "Why is it better if he stays here?"

"'Cuz I know he's okay."

Dan felt a shaft of guilt that made his entire chest hurt. Had he made things worse for this child by injecting himself into her life? But being friends with Lena, he couldn't have avoided it, except by being less nice. He wasn't that kind of person, and he had quickly come to love Krystal. So what now? He looked almost desperately at Vicki, who was frowning faintly.

"Time for therapy," she murmured.

"What's that?" Krys asked.

Vicki didn't answer and Krys finished her snack. Then she threw her arms around Dan before slipping off his lap. "Take me to bed," she demanded.

So Dan, with a nod from Vicki, did exactly that, wondering what kind of hell he'd stirred up for Vicki and Krystal.

Vicki waited downstairs, pacing from the kitchen across the foyer, through the living room and back again. There was no question what was going on with Krystal now, and it wasn't just the move. She was grasping the fact that the father she barely remembered had gone away and he wasn't okay anymore.

Understanding had been inevitable. Maybe her anxiety was, as well. Maybe this was perfectly normal coping, but Vicki felt desperate for a second opinion. She'd unleashed something with this move. Or maybe it would have happened, anyway. How the hell could she know?

But it seemed to be Dan that Krys was worrying about. Not her friends back in Austin, not Lena going away for a weekend. Krys's concern seemed specifically focused on Dan and her mother. This was no generalized anxiety. The child seemed worried about just two people.

Inevitably, Vicki wondered if seeing Dan in uniform had exacerbated the problem. But then in fairness she had to admit that it had started the first night they'd been here, just as she was leaving Krys's bedroom. If anything had stirred it up, it had been the move. It had just reached out to include Dan, as well.

Vicki heard him coming down the stairs. "Sound asleep," he said as he reached the bottom. "Vicki—"

She waved her hand. "This isn't about you. It started the day we moved here. Maybe it just needs to happen. Sooner or later she had to deal with the fact that

Hal would never come back. Maybe she's just getting to a point where she can adequately express her fear."

"Maybe." He hesitated. "Was she worried about Lena going for the weekend?"

"She never mentioned it."

"Then I'm a problem."

Vicki rounded on him, trying to keep her voice low so as not to wake Krystal. "You're not the problem. The problem is a murdering SOB who took that girl's father away. The problem is me moving her halfway across the country. She's learning that sometimes things go away for good. The question is how to deal with it, because much as it stinks, Dan, it's reality. It's life. Everything goes away eventually. You and I know that. Now she does, too."

Vicki resumed pacing. He finally got out of her way by sitting on the bottom steps. "Talk to me," he said quietly.

"I worked for years with kids near her age. I saw it all the time. They have a full complement of emotions to deal with. Anyone who dismisses a child's feelings is a fool. They're real. They're huge. The problem is that a child doesn't have the means of expressing them completely. Or sometimes even a way to identify them."

"And a therapist can do that? Better than you?"

"A good one with training, of course. I'm a teacher. That's a whole different bailiwick." She settled at last on a chair in the kitchen with a fresh cup of coffee. He joined her. "A therapist would get her to act out the things she can't put into words. Dealing with them in nonthreatening ways could be helpful."

"Then I guess that's what you need to do. I know

we have some psychologists in town, but I can't evaluate them."

Vicki put her elbows on the table and her chin in her hand. "You need your sleep. I'm perfectly capable of worrying on my own."

"Hey," he said. "You don't have to worry alone, and if you think I'm walking out of here after everything that's happened, you're crazy. I'm staying. Live with it."

She gave him a wan smile. "Okay." Then she closed her eyes. "I may be making too much of this. It wouldn't be the first time. I was thinking that sooner or later she was going to deal with her loss in some way, and I guess this is it."

"But you're sure I'm not making it worse?"

Vicki's eyes popped open. "No, you're not. She's worrying about me, too. What are you and I supposed to do? Desert her? Hardly. She's afraid of losing *us*. That's what we need to deal with, and the only way to make it worse is to withdraw in some way."

"Okay." He nodded. "But then there's you. I shouldn't have made love to you. You already told me your feelings about cops, and I should have kept a safe distance. Damn it, Vicki, you've got enough on your plate to worry about without adding me to the equation."

"Too late, cowboy."

"Ah, hell, how often do I have to hint to you that this isn't a dangerous job? Do you have a computer? Look up the ten most dangerous jobs. Cops don't even make the list. You'd have more to worry about if I were a logger."

"I'm starting to realize that," she admitted. "Gut

emotional reactions don't give way easily to reason, though."

"No," he agreed with a sigh.

Just then thunder rumbled loudly, vibrating the entire house. Both of them instinctively looked up.

"With any luck," Dan said, "we'll be rained out tomorrow."

She eyed him curiously, noting again how sexy he was. Even now, in the midst of all this concern about Krys, she was noting that. Broad shoulders, strong face, warm eyes... God, she had the bug bad. She'd have liked nothing more than to forget everything in his arms right now. She dragged her thoughts back into line. "You want the games to be canceled?"

"Now I do. I don't want to be away from you two that long. That's me talking, not Krys, by the way. I'm in danger of developing some separation anxiety of my own over you girls."

If she hadn't been in such a confused and worried state, Vicki might have laughed. It was such a sweet admission for him to make, though. "Thank you, Dan."

Thunder rolled again, and the house shook once more. Dan pulled out his cell phone, tapped it a couple times. "Bad weather but no tornado warning. Thunderstorms through tomorrow afternoon."

"There go the games."

"The fields will turn to mud if we try to play." He set his phone on the table. "Assuming it rains. And we can't play if there's any danger of lightning."

Almost as if the heavens heard him, they opened up. Even from the ground floor, the rain sounded loud and heavy.

"Question answered," Vicki said.

"Yeah. By the way, a cop is three times more likely to get struck by lightning than die in the line of duty."

Her head jerked a little. Why had he said that? But she knew why. Oh, yes, she knew. He was trying to reach past her emotional resistance to his profession. Gently, persistently, he just kept working at it.

After their lovemaking, she had begun to think resistance was futile. She wanted him again. And then again. At no foreseeable time did she want Dan to back out of her life. She guessed that meant she was already in trouble.

"I told Krys I was going to sleep on the couch. I hope that was okay."

"Of course." Vicki decided that she had to put an end to this evening now. She had a great deal of thinking to do, all because she'd made love with him, and because of Krys's reaction to his leaving.

Vicki would be surprised if she slept at all.

In the morning, the storm showed no sign of abating. The games were officially postponed. Dan took over the kitchen, making pancakes and chatting with Krys as she sat at the table, coloring industriously. She was currently fascinated by coloring books that featured tropical fish.

Vicki doubted that nature, for all its love of color, had created anything like what Krystal produced. At least the colors were bright and cheerful, she thought as she admired the two that Krys had already completed.

At some point Dan must have darted back to his place, because he'd exchanged last night's sweatshirt for a green one.

Soon a platter piled with small pancakes sat in the

middle of the table. Vicki helped Krys with the butter and syrup, then helped herself. Dan poured more coffee and joined them.

Such a perfectly normal scene, Vicki thought. Like an ordinary family sitting around a breakfast table. But last night had blown up her illusions. She was getting seriously involved with a man who was a cop, and Krys had attached herself to him like a limpet. Worst of all, Vicki's own uneasiness about herself had been completely swamped by her concerns about her daughter.

She felt a momentary burst of resentment, then banished it. Sure, it would be nice if she could just revel in memories of what she and Dan had shared last night, if she could just look forward to spending the day and another night with him, acting like giddy kids in the first throes of a relationship.

But that wasn't going to happen, and she felt shame for resenting it even for a moment. She wasn't a kid any longer, and she had a daughter who needed to be her top priority at all times. But Vicki was also human, as her all-too-frequent mistakes made abundantly clear. She had committed herself and her daughter to a path that might not have been the wisest choice.

But back in Austin, even with all the concerned friends, she had felt a deep emptiness inside. At first she had put it down to missing Hal, but as time passed she'd realized she desperately needed to try to find a normal life. She had a lot of years ahead of her, and much as she missed Hal, living them out as his widow forever wasn't going to satisfy anything else inside her. She needed other things, a life that didn't exist only in the past, or in the immediate moment when something needed her attention. She needed a future to look forward to, beyond watching her daughter grow up.

Was that a crime? Of course not, but sometimes her emotions made her feel like a traitor. Then she wondered why. The life she had once planned with Hal was gone. All those desires needed to be replaced somehow.

She watched Dan and Krys laughing about something, and felt an ache for all she had lost, but also felt the beauty of the moment. Krys moved ahead almost fearlessly, making new connections, coming to care for new people. She wasn't afraid of putting her heart out there. But she did fear losses.

Vicki took a hard look at herself and wondered if she was less courageous than a four-year-old. Krys had left everything behind, too, when they moved here. And to this day Vicki honestly didn't know how much Krys missed her father. Or how much she remembered him, apart from photographs. Surely some of her sense of security had been affected, but Vicki wondered if the move up here, which had started all those pleas for people not to go away, might be the real source of Krys's anxiety. It was recent, a fresh wound, and might be the whole problem.

Yet Krys had never asked to go back to Austin. Overall, she seemed to be happy here. And Vicki was spinning in circles, wondering what she could do about any of this now.

Dan leaned toward Krys. "I need to go home and shower and change. Is that okay?"

Vicki held her breath. Then, to her amazement, Krys nodded. "Okay."

Dan smiled. "I won't be long, pumpkin."

"We'll do the dishes," Vicki announced—cheerfully,

she hoped. Had they just crossed a hurdle? Would it last?

"Save some for me." Dan grinned. "I made quite a mess."

"Ah, but you cooked," Vicki retorted, managing a smile of sorts.

Dan walked out, the front door closed behind him, and Vicki felt herself on tenterhooks again. But Krystal didn't react negatively at all. She slid off her chair and carried the first plate to the sink. "Let's go, Mommy."

Dan took far longer than was necessary for a shower and change. Vicki wondered if he was testing the waters...or if he needed some escape. Certainly, he hadn't had a moment to do things his way since walking in here yesterday. He needed some space. Who wouldn't?

But the thought made her glum, even though she scolded herself for being unreasonable. The man had a life. He had things to do. No reason she and Krys should just take over his every waking moment, apart from his job.

Then she wondered if he'd gotten a call. At once her heart slipped into high gear. Could he be responding to a dangerous situation right now? What if he never came back?

She glanced at the clock. It really hadn't been that long. She was overreacting and being unfair, all at once. Krys had resumed her coloring, and asked if purple and orange went together.

"If you want them to," Vicki answered a bit absently.

Finally, the phone rang. She jumped to answer it. "Hey," said Dan's warm voice. "Sorry, but I have to go into work. It should be only a couple of hours."

Vicki glanced at the clock, setting a timer in herself even though she knew it was foolish. "Okay." She bit back the question about whether it was dangerous.

"Want me to explain to Krys?"

"She seems okay right now. Coloring."

"Leave well enough alone. Be back as soon as I can."

She hung up and looked at her daughter. "Dan had to go to work for a little while."

Krys nodded, and Vicki felt a huge wave of relief, as no crises or disturbances seemed to ensue. The only thing that drew Krys out of her preoccupation was loud rumbling from the sky.

"I don't like thunder," she said decisively.

"Really? I do." Vicki sat with her at the table.

Krys eyed her. "Crazy" was her pronouncement, and despite fears that were determined to nibble at Vicki, she had to laugh.

"Maybe I am," she agreed. Lately, she was wondering if that was a serious possibility.

At noon, Dan still hadn't returned. By then Vicki was trying to keep a leash on major anxiety. When the phone rang, she flew to pick it up.

"Hi," said the familiar voice of Janine Dalrymple. "Can I come over and steal Krys?"

Her mind had been so far away that Vicki blinked and had to replay the question in her head. "Steal her?"

"The only thing more tiring than two four-year-olds having a good time together is one of them creating trouble out of boredom," Janine said wryly. "Help? I'll pick up Krys and they can have some playtime over here for a few hours."

Krys wanted to go. Vicki knew a moment's surprise,

then wondered why. Of course Krys wanted to play with Peggy. Her daughter showed no signs of wanting to check out on normal life. What she did show was separation anxiety, but only sometimes. Vicki guessed she'd wait and see for a while before hunting for a therapist. If the problem didn't ease, or if it grew, she'd take action, but right now a lot of this could be explained by the move. Whatever bugged Krys from time to time, it certainly wasn't bugging her today.

So a half hour later, Krys left with Peggy and Janine, bouncing happily as she went out the door.

Which left Vicki alone with a clock. A couple hours? It had already been four.

The nightmare slammed her—the nightmare of Hal's delayed return from the convenience store, followed later, much later, by the arrival of the department chaplain and a couple of Hal's friends. The News.

She paced almost insanely, arguing with herself. The job had just taken longer than expected. Dan was no kid, having to report in every time he got delayed. She was overreacting. Nothing had happened.

But deep inside, she didn't believe it. She couldn't. Something terrible was wrong.

Chapter Ten

Janine called at four. "If you don't mind, I'm keeping Krys for the night. The girls are happy and have already built a tent in the living room they want to sleep in. If Krys has any problem or gets homesick, I'll call you and bring her home."

Vicki's instinct was to say no. She wanted Krys at her side right now. She needed to touch her, see her, be sure she was all right. The need grew proportionately with her fears about Dan.

But she caught herself, tried to speak calmly with Krys, and when she realized her daughter really wanted to spend the night, she agreed. It was a good step for her.

Even if it was hell for Vicki.

All the day's stress overwhelmed her, exhausting her. Finally numb, she collapsed on the couch, trying so hard not to think about what the next knock on the door might bring.

Starkly, she faced the fact that if something had happened to Dan it was going to hurt every bit as much as her loss of Hal. No amount of arguing with herself could change that.

She faced something else in those long hours, too. She faced the loss of Hal, and the near loss of Krys to a maniac driver, and accepted at last that it was impossible to care without taking the risks that went with it. Nobody could escape that.

But understanding didn't ease her fretfulness. Loving meant risking, and now Vicki faced her demons all over again.

Numerous times she thought of calling Dan just to be sure he was okay, but stopped herself. Hal had long ago explained that calls while he was working might distract him at exactly the wrong moment.

But when Dan had called that morning, he'd made it sound so much as if this would be routine. A couple hours. They were well past that and then some.

Anxiety made her skin crawl, and inside she could feel herself bracing for the blow of bad news. What the hell had she been thinking, letting another cop into her heart?

She had known him such a short time. How had he come to mean so much? And now, with Krystal so engaged, there was no way to back out of this. It had happened, and this rock was rolling all the way down to the bottom of the hill.

Vicki almost hated herself as she watched the minutes tick by, so slowly that time seemed nearly to stop. She'd dropped her guard and done the very thing she had vowed never to do again. How had she been so stupid? The anticipated pain was already shredding her.

Then she heard the front door open. She stood up, ready for disaster, but instead saw Dan. He was still in uniform, and the sight almost made her sick. A cop. A damn cop.

"Vicki?" Evidently, he could read something on her face. He paused on the threshold of the living room, hands at his side, worry creasing his brow.

"You…you…" Words failed her and she flew at him. His hands caught her elbows, but that didn't stop her from pounding his chest. "I was scared," she cried, the entire day's worry pouring out of her. "So scared! Where the hell were you?"

He caught her hands, stopping her blows. "Easy," he said quietly.

"Easy? How can I be easy? Damn you, I've been waiting for news and…" She choked and tears began to flood her cheeks.

"I'm sorry," he said, keeping his voice quiet. "I'm sorry. I was out of phone range and it went on longer…"

"You could have died and I wouldn't even have known!"

He wrapped his arms around her, pinning her arms to his sides, turning into a strong but gentle straitjacket. "I was safe. We were looking for a lost little girl…"

"That makes me feel better how?" But her tears renewed, and along with them came hiccups. Then, with shocking abruptness, she realized she was acting like a wild woman. The shock froze her and everything within her.

Strong arms surrounded her protectively, and at last, at long last, the tension seeped out of her. Reason made a steady return. Still crying, but more quietly, Vicki sagged in Dan's arms and rested her head on his chest. He was here. He was safe.

"It's okay," he murmured repeatedly. "It's okay. Next time things run over, I'll make sure you get a call."

That made her feel foolish. She had no claim on this man, certainly not one that justified a leash on him. Fear had ripped her for hours, and now all she could feel was painful relief. She felt shredded inside, but reason returned. She drew ragged breaths, seeking her voice, finding it. Rustily, she said, "I'm sorry."

"No need. But where's Krys?"

Vicki heard the concern in Dan's voice and it struck her that she had given no thought to what *he* might fear. Could she have been any more selfish? She sucked in more air. "She's fine. She went to Peggy's for the night."

"That's a relief," he admitted. Loosening his hold on her, he raised a hand to stroke Vicki's hair. "All day long I wondered what you were dealing with when I didn't get back."

"Now you know," she said brokenly. "Krys is fine and I'm falling to pieces. Sorry."

"Don't be."

He shifted his hold and lifted her from her feet, carrying her to the couch, where he sat with her on his lap. For a long time, he simply cradled her, scattering kisses on her head, stroking her arm, letting the storm pass.

Eventually, when her heart stopped aching, she said, "I went off the deep end."

"I can't imagine why."

She scrubbed her face with her sleeve, then leaned

back a bit to look at him. Oddly, or so it seemed to her, he looked fairly happy. "You mad at me?" she asked.

"For what? I knew you had to be worrying. I was afraid Krys was freaking out, and I couldn't even get a satellite connection with my radio. We were in the woods, hunting for this girl, and the storm…well, it killed our comms. We were reduced to tracking each other with whistles."

"Did you find her?"

"The dogs did. God knows how with all this rain, but they did. Poor kid, she was hypothermic, nearly blue. She's in the hospital now, but I hear she'll be okay."

"Thank God."

"Yeah. Thank God. Now let's stop worrying about her and talk about you."

Vicki shook her head and burrowed her face into his shoulder. "I went off the deep end, as I said. I'm not proud of it."

"You shouldn't be ashamed, either. Although next time you want to pound your fists on my chest, could you avoid the badge and the name plate?" He sounded amused.

She jerked back. "I hurt you? I hurt you. Let me see."

He shook his head. "Just some small bruises. Kinda painful when it was happening, though."

She felt so ashamed. But that didn't stop her from reaching for his shirt buttons. Unfortunately, he had a T-shirt underneath. "Damn it," she said.

He laughed. "Really, do you see any blood? I'm fine."

"Dan…"

He shifted her off his lap. "Okay, okay. Need to get rid of this damn gun belt, anyway." He pulled it off, placing it on a table, then shucked both his shirts. "See, I'm whole."

But she could see the red spots where she had hammered the clasps into him. "I'm so sorry," she whispered. "I never hit anybody before. I'm so ashamed, Dan."

"Cut it out. I'm kind of flattered that you cared that much. And believe me, I know what you were thinking."

"I left thinking behind hours ago," she admitted. She scrubbed her face again, trying to get rid of the last stickiness from her tears.

He squatted in front of her, clasping her hands. "I need to go over to my place to change. My pants are still full of burrs. And I don't want my gun in this house whenever Krys comes back. At home I can lock it up. Do you want to come with me or will you be okay for a little while?"

She wanted to go with him. So far she'd never seen his house. On the other hand, she needed to prove something to herself and to him, that she could be okay when he was away. That she wasn't going to be a constant burden demanding to know his whereabouts every minute of the day.

"You go," she said. "I think I'll clean up, too."

He leaned forward and kissed her. "Not long this time, I promise."

Back at his own place, Dan locked his gun belt in the armored box he kept for just that purpose, then put it back on the high shelf. It felt good to get out of his wet clothes, and he spent some time pulling burrs out of his pants. Then he tossed them aside, deciding that could wait. He needed to get back to Vicki.

And if today had taught him one thing, it was that his need for her was pretty strong. Being away from her, busy though he had been, had been tough. He'd missed her, and worried about her and Krys damn near every second.

He'd hoped he'd come back to find everything was okay, but he hadn't. Evidently Krys was fine, but her mother had had a major freak-out. He couldn't blame her for that, not given what had happened with Hal.

But as he stepped into the shower, Dan realized that he could no longer just let things between them drift along. He knew she was resistant to his job, so he hadn't really pressed her in any way, but today had written an entirely different story.

Not only had he missed the woman all day long, but apparently she'd been anxious enough about him to turn into a wild woman when she saw he was safe. She must have been pumped on adrenaline and fear the entire day. They had to talk about that, because unless she could deal with this, they'd have to part ways.

The thought speared him painfully. He knew how much he cared about her, but he couldn't do this to her repeatedly. That would be selfish. Maybe he'd been selfish from the outset. She'd told him about her worries during her marriage to Hal, and he'd been smug enough to wonder if she'd exaggerated them in the aftermath of his death. Well, Hal had died, and Vicki clearly bore the scars of that trauma. How they were going to get past that, he didn't know.

He showered in hot water, then toweled himself briskly, glad to feel warm again. It wasn't a cold day, just a cool one, but the rain hadn't helped. At last, in fresh jeans and a wool shirt, he pulled on a jacket and headed next door. Dread dogged his steps, because the two of them had something to work out, and they couldn't let it drag on. It wouldn't be fair to any of them.

He let himself in, and smelled coffee from the kitchen. Like a hound, he followed the aroma and found Vicki seated at the table, with a mug in front of her and a coffee cake. She was freshly showered, with her hair beginning to curl all over her head.

"You must be starved," she said brightly. "I can make us dinner shortly."

But he wasn't deceived. She might be smiling and acting as if nothing had happened, but they both knew better. Something had happened, all right, and it was momentous. Just how momentous remained to be seen.

He grabbed a mug of coffee and sat next to her. "The first time I saw you," he said, "you peeked out the door to see who Krys was talking to."

"I remember." Vicki smiled faintly.

"You looked tired, but that wasn't what struck me."

"No?"

"No. I thought you were one of the most beautiful women I'd ever seen."

She caught her breath, then her smile widened. "Wow."

He wondered if he was going to make a mess of this. His heart began to beat more heavily, and for the first time in a long time he felt fear. Not the fear that sometimes happened on the job. Not the fear he'd felt for that little girl today. No, this was personal. This was Dan Casey's happiness on the line.

"Vicki, I can't do this again to you. Today, I mean. I put you through hell. No one has the right to do that. But I'm a cop. I'll continue to be a cop. This job is part of me. It's in my blood."

She nodded, her smile fading. "I didn't ask you to quit."

"No, you never did. But I understand why you don't like it, and if I didn't get it before, I sure as hell got it this afternoon."

He thought she flushed faintly, but he couldn't be sure. "I'm sorry," she said again.

"Don't keep apologizing. This is reality, and that's part of it. You were terrified, and I can't blame you for that. But neither of us is going to change, so maybe it would be best if I just kind of eased away. I'll still be friends with Krys. I love her to death. But no matter how hard I try, there are going to be days like this. I can ask the dispatcher to give you a call if I'm gone longer than expected, and explain what's going on, when I can't reach you, but this is a big county and there are plenty of places where communications fail. So there *will* be days like this again. I don't have the right to ask that of you."

She nodded and looked down into her mug. Now his heart was sinking. This was it, and today he'd faced the fact that losing her was going to be as hard as losing Callie.

Vicki was quiet for so long, he wondered if he should just get up and leave. But then she sighed and reached out her hand. He took it and their fingers twined.

"I was terrified today," she admitted. "Then I acted like a madwoman when I found out you were okay. That makes no sense, does it?"

"Actually, it does. But go on." His heart was already hurting.

"The thing is, Dan, what difference does it make if you walk away for good, or die?"

The question caught him sideways. He was still trying to be sure he understood when she continued speaking.

"However I lose you, it's going to be hell," she said. "I figured that out. And I figured out that you were right when you once told me that you wouldn't have traded a single minute with Callie to avoid the pain. I wouldn't give up a single minute with Hal. So why should I give up a single moment with you? If you want me, that is. Because loss is inevitable for everyone. The end comes. And I finally realized that what matters is the journey. A week, a month, fifty years. It's the journey, not the end."

She lifted her gaze, meeting his. "I don't want to trade any moments with you to avoid what could happen tomorrow or what might never happen."

His grip on her hand tightened. "You're sure?"

"I had plenty of time today to relive hell. I may have to do it again. But… I don't want to lose you, and certainly not for that reason."

His voice cracked a little as he said, "I love you, Vicki. I am so hugely in love with you. You can handle that?"

She smiled. "I hope so, because terror taught me a lesson today. I'm so in love with you that it hurts. I don't want to live without you."

He watched the joy grow on her face, and felt the answer in his own heart. "Just promise you won't hide your fears from me," he asked. "That would be bad for both of us. I can handle it if you can."

"Okay." But she was still glowing. He hoped he never caused that glow to vanish. But another need was growing in him.

"I want to take you upstairs," he said. "Make love to you until neither of us can move."

"Oh, yes," she breathed, leaning toward him. Then she startled him by straightening. "Krys. I'd better phone her and make sure she still wants to spend the night. Otherwise she might call when…"

Vicki's blush enchanted him and heightened his hunger for her. "Call," he said, much as he didn't want to wait to sweep her to bed, where he could show her in the best way possible how much he adored her.

So Vicki got the phone and soon was speaking to Krys. She had to hold the receiver away from her ear, and even Dan could hear the excitement and words tripping over each other. Then Vicki handed the phone to him.

"Hey, pumpkin," he said warmly. "How's it going?" He wound up laughing as he listened to Krys talking about tents and blankets, and a movie and…well, pretty soon he lost track of it all. It was wonderful just to hear her so happy.

When he said goodbye, there were no words about him not going away. Relief swelled his heart even more.

Thunder rumbled hollowly as he led Vicki upstairs. There was no moonlight tonight, so she turned on the small lamp beside her bed. In its golden glow, they made love slowly, learning each other as they hadn't the last time, savoring every touch and kiss and newly discovered delight.

She was perfect, he thought, and he ran his hands along her, from her breasts to her thighs. Perfect. He wouldn't have changed one thing about her, not even the mole he found on her hip. Her hands traced his contours in the same way, building the fire between them until everything vanished.

When he entered her, he knew he'd come home. And when he toppled over the summit with her, the explosion seemed to sear him, wiping away old scars and leaving him whole again.

They slept fitfully that night, making love lazily or desperately as the mood struck. But finally Vicki awoke from a dreamless sleep to see the sunlight of a new day filling her room.

"Good morning."

She turned a bit and found Dan watching her with a smile. She stretched and smiled back.

"You keep doing that and we're going to still be here when Krys gets back."

She sat up. "Krys!"

"Janine's bringing her in a few minutes. I was trying to decide whether to let you sleep, but the fact is, if I answer the door, the whole town is going to be talking. Which isn't a big deal, if you want to marry me."

Her breath lodged in her throat. Joy exploded in her chest like a million fireworks. "Is that a proposal?"

"Seems like," he said. "You don't have to answer right now. Just think about it."

Then he swung out of the bed and began to toss clothes to her. "I guess there's another lady I need to ask, too. Assuming you say yes."

Her hands were shaking as she donned the jeans

and blue T-shirt he'd found for her. He pulled on what he'd worn last night. How could she not say yes? Of course she was going to say yes. She couldn't imagine life without Dan anymore. Her heart overflowed with happiness, and as long as Krys didn't have a problem…

Vicki looked at Dan. "I've got to ask Krys first." Not that she really wondered how Krys would react. Her attachment to Dan was as plain as a neon sign.

He nodded. "I guess that's an indirect yes from you." Then he grinned.

Vicki struggled with the zipper on her jeans. "I can't believe I didn't hear the phone."

"I can. You were zonked. If I weren't programmed to wake up from a coma at the sound of the phone, I'd have missed it, too."

He grabbed her and spun her around quickly, saying, "I never thought I'd be this happy again." He gave her a quick kiss before turning toward the stairs. "Mmm," he said. "Trouble's brewing if we stay here. Let's go."

She was laughing as she hurried downstairs. She could hear Janine's car pulling into the drive.

"I'll make coffee," Dan said.

Vicki answered the door and found Janine standing there with Krys, who was pulling her small overnight suitcase.

"They had a wonderful time," Janine said. "I don't think they slept two winks."

"Want to come in for coffee?"

"Another time. I've got one very tired Peggy, and I'm hoping that when I get home we can both have a nap. We'll do this again soon."

Krystal entered the foyer with somewhat less energy than usual. Vicki waved at Janine as she pulled away, then closed the door and looked at her daughter, taking in the obvious signs of fatigue. "Good fun, huh?"

"Yup," Krys answered. Her T-shirt looked rumpled from being slept in, and her hair was only partly brushed. Her eyelids drooped a little before suddenly widening. Then she cocked her head, dropped the handle of her suitcase and beelined for the kitchen. "Dan!"

When Vicki entered the room, she saw Krys in Dan's arms as he stood at the counter. He held out one arm, inviting her into the hug.

Nothing could be more perfect, Vicki thought as she leaned into him and hugged her little girl. Somehow one move and one man had brought her a joy she had thought she would never know again. The painful past seemed to recede more with each moment.

Krys looped one arm around Dan's neck and the other around Vicki's. "I was lonesome for you."

"I was lonesome for you, too," Vicki said.

"Me, too," Dan agreed. "But you had a lot of fun?"

"Yup." Krys beamed. "Peggy's great. She still has a daddy and he's funny."

Vicki's heart lurched. She looked at Dan and found him watching her. He seemed not to want to step on her toes or something. That had to change.

"Let's sit on the sofa," Vicki said. "Dan and I want to ask you something important."

Soon they were sitting with Krys between them. She looked from one to the other. "Was I bad?"

"Heavens, no!" Vicki said. "You weren't bad at all. This is about something else."

"Good."

But how to begin this conversation? Once again she sent a silent appeal to Dan. He tilted his head a bit, as if he were reluctant to start, but realized the duty had fallen to him.

"Krys?"

She turned to him.

"I want to marry your mother. Do you like that idea?"

Krys surprised Vicki. "Does Mommy want to marry you?"

"Yes," Vicki said. "I do."

"Does that mean Dan will be my daddy?"

Vicki's heart nearly stopped. Her throat jammed up, leaving her unable to speak. Dan reached out and lifted Krys onto his lap. "I will be your daddy if that's what you want. Is it?"

Krys didn't hesitate a beat. "Yup," she said decisively. "You're a good daddy."

"Wow," Dan murmured. "Um, just wow."

Krys then looked at Vicki with a tired but happy smile. "I picked him, Mommy."

Vicki guessed she had. She dissolved into laughter, and Dan joined her.

"So can I have a baby brother or sister, too?"

Dan's and Vicki's gazes locked. "That's entirely possible," they both said at the same moment.

"And I want to be a flower girl."

Dan hugged her tight. "You're going to be one very special flower girl."

"Good." Then, between one breath and the next, she dozed off in Dan's arms.

Vicki felt tears of happiness prickle her eyes, and thought Dan's eyes shone, as well.

"That was easy," he murmured.

"Well," said Vicki, "she picked you." And then she

added something that seemed as important to her as all the mountains and valleys she had traveled since moving here. "And I guess I picked you, too."

He smiled, adjusting Krys on his lap so he could draw Vicki up against him and hug her. "I am one hell of a lucky guy."

Vicki smiled, truly happy, content and at peace for the first time in forever. The shadows would return sometimes, and storms might come, but she no longer feared them. They would weather them as they'd weathered everything else, but this time they'd get through them together.

A bright new future had begun.

Epilogue

They were married just before Christmas in Good Shepherd Church. Krystal got to be a flower girl, and at her insistence, so did Peggy. The little girls scattered bright red petals down the aisle ahead of Vicki, who walked on the arm of her late husband's best friend, Bill Hanton. Her attention was fixed on Dan, resplendent in a blue suit. She herself wore blue velvet, rather than the traditional white. Dan loved her in blue.

The pews were filled with her new friends, a lot of deputies and their families, some teachers, Lena's friends. Many of Hal's old friends from Austin had made the trip, too, resplendent in their dress uniforms, prepared to provide an honor guard a little later. This time Vicki was happy to see the blue wall gathered around her, and they looked as thrilled for her as she was.

Inside her, still a secret from everyone but Dan, a new child was growing. Ahead of her lay her new life, and she was being ushered there by Hal's closest friend. Joy filled her heart to overflowing.

When Bill placed her hand in Dan's, she felt almost as if it was a changing of the guard. Dan broke tradition a bit, drawing Krys to stand between him and Vicki.

Lena, grinning from ear to ear, stood as maid of honor for her, and gave her a little nudge as if to say "You go, girl."

Krys had gone to therapy, but hadn't needed much of it. Not for months now had she expressed any anxiety over anyone leaving. Vicki felt she had overcome the worst of her own fears, and faced the future with excitement and pleasure.

"I love you," Dan whispered to her, just before the minister began the ceremony.

"I love you, too."

Smiling, they faced the pastor, ready to embark on a new journey.

* * * * *

Don't miss Rachel Lee's next romance,
PLAYING WITH FIRE,
available August 2015 from
Harlequin Romantic Suspense!

SPECIAL EXCERPT FROM

HQN™

*McKenzie Shaw works harder than anyone as the
mayor of her hometown, Haven Point. But all
of her hard work might be for nothing when her
long-ago crush, Ben Kilpatrick, shows up again,
about to wreak havoc in Haven Point—and on
McKenzie's heart.*

*Read on for a sneak preview of
REDEMPTION BAY,
the latest book in* New York Times *bestselling
author RaeAnne Thayne's heartwarming series,
HAVEN POINT.
On sale now!*

THIS WAS HER favorite kind of Haven Point evening.

McKenzie Shaw locked the front door of her shop, Point Made Flowers and Gifts. The day had been long and hectic, filled with customers and orders, which was wonderful, but also plenty of unavoidable mayoral business.

She was tired and wanted to stretch out on the terrace or her beloved swing, with her feet up and something cool at her elbow. The image beckoned but the sweetness of the view in front of her made her pause.

"Hold on," she said to Paprika, her cinnamon standard poodle. The dog gave her a long-suffering look but settled next to the bench in front of the store.

McKenzie sat and reached a hand down to pet Rika's curly hair. A few sailboats cut through the stunning blue waters of Lake Haven, silvery and bright in the fading light, with the rugged, snowcapped mountains as a backdrop.

She didn't stop nearly often enough to soak in the beautiful view or enjoy the June evening air, tart and clean from the mighty fir and pines growing in abundance around the lake.

A tourist couple walked past holding hands and eating gelato cones from Carmela's, their hair backlit into golden halos by the setting sun. From a short distance away, she could hear children laughing and shrieking as they played on the beach at the city park and the alluring scent of grilling steak somewhere close by made her stomach grumble.

She loved every season here on the lake but the magnificent Haven Point summers were her favorite—especially lazy summer evenings filled with long shadows and spectacular sunsets.

Kayaking on the lake, watching children swim out to the floating docks, seeing old-timers in ancient boats casting gossamer lines out across the water. It was all part of the magic of Haven Point's short summer season.

The town heavily depended on the influx of tourists during the summer, though it didn't come close to the crowds enjoyed by their larger city to the north, Shelter Springs—especially since the Haven Point Inn burned down just before Christmas and had yet to be rebuilt.

Shelter Springs had more available lodging, more restaurants, more shopping—as well as more problems with parking, traffic congestion and crime, she reminded herself.

"Evening, Mayor," Mike Bailey called, waving as

he rumbled past the store in the gorgeous old blue '57 Chevy pickup he'd restored.

She waved back, then nodded to Luis Ayala, locking up his insurance agency across the street.

A soft, warm feeling of contentment seeped through her. This was her town, these were her people. She was part of it, just like the Redemption Mountains across the lake. She had fought to earn that sense of belonging since the day she showed up, a lost, grieving, bewildered girl.

She had worked hard to earn the respect of her friends and neighbors. The chance to serve as the mayor had never been something she sought but she had accepted the challenge willingly. It wasn't about power or influence—not that one could find much of either in a small town like Haven Point. She simply wanted to do anything she could to make a difference in her community. She wanted to think she was serving with honor and dignity, but she was fully aware there were plenty in town who might disagree.

Her stomach growled, louder this time. That steak smelled as if it was charred to perfection. Too bad she didn't know who was grilling it or she might just stop by to say hello. McKenzie was briefly tempted to stop in at Serrano's or even grab a gelato of her own at Carmela's—stracciatella, her particular favorite—but she decided she would be better off taking Rika home.

"Come on, girl. Let's go."

The dog jumped to her feet, all eager, lanky grace, and McKenzie gripped the leash and headed off.

She lived not quite a mile from her shop downtown and she and Rika both looked forward all day to this evening walk along the trail that circled the lake.

As she walked, she waved at people walking, biking, driving, even boating past when the shoreline came into view. It was quite a workout for her arm but she didn't mind. Each wave was another reminder that this was her town and she loved it.

"Let's grill some chicken when we get home," she said aloud to Rika, whose tongue lolled out with appropriate enthusiasm.

Talking to her dog again. Not a good sign but she decided it was too beautiful an evening to worry about her decided lack of any social life to speak of. Town council meetings absolutely didn't count.

WHEN SHE REACHED her lakeside house, however, she discovered a luxury SUV with California plates in the driveway of the house next to hers, with boat trailer and gleaming wooden boat attached.

Great.

Apparently someone had rented the Sloane house.

Normally she would be excited about new neighbors but in this case, she knew the tenants would only be temporary. Since moving to Shelter Springs, Carole Sloane-Hall had been renting out the house she received as a settlement in her divorce for a furnished vacation rental. Sometimes people stayed for a week or two, sometimes only a few days.

It was a lovely home, probably one of the most luxurious lakefront rentals within the city limits. Though not large, it had huge windows overlooking the lake, a wide flagstone terrace and a semiprivate boat dock—which, unfortunately, was shared between McKenzie's own property and Carole's rental house.

She wouldn't let it spoil her evening, she told herself. Usually the renters were very nice people, quiet and polite. She generally tried to act as friendly and welcoming as possible.

It wouldn't bother her at all except the two properties had virtually an open backyard because both needed access to the shared dock, with only some landscaping between the houses that ended several yards from the high watermark. Sometimes she found the lack of privacy a little disconcerting, with strangers temporarily living next door, but Carole assured her she planned to put the house on the market at the end of the summer. With everything else McKenzie had to worry about, she had relegated the vacation rental situation next door to a distant corner of her brain.

New neighbors or not, though, she still adored her own house. She had purchased it two years earlier and still felt a little rush of excitement when she unlocked the front door and walked over the threshold.

Over those two years, she had worked hard to make it her own, sprucing it up with new paint, taking down a few walls and adding one in a better spot. The biggest expense had been for the renovated master bath, which now contained a huge claw-foot tub, and the new kitchen with warm travertine countertops and the intricately tiled backsplash she had done herself.

This was hers and she loved every inch of it, almost more than she loved her little store downtown.

She walked through to the back door and let Rika off her leash. Though the yard was only fenced on one side, just as the Sloane house was fenced on the corresponding outer property edge, Rika was well trained and never left the yard.

Her cell phone rang as she was throwing together a quick lemon-tarragon marinade for the chicken.

Some days, she wanted to grab her kayak, paddle out to the middle of Lake Haven—where it was rumored to be so deep, the bottom had never been truly charted—and toss the stupid thing overboard.

This time when she saw the caller ID, she smiled, wiped her hands on a dish towel and quickly answered. "Hey, Devin."

"Hey, sis. I can't believe you're holding out on me! Come on. Doesn't your favorite sister get to be among the first to hear?"

She tucked the phone in her shoulder and returned to cutting the lemon for the marinade as she mentally reviewed her day for anything spill-worthy to her sister.

The store had been busy enough. She had busted the doddering and not-quite-right Mrs. Anglesey for trying to walk out of the store without paying for the pretty hand-beaded bracelet she tried on when she came into the store with her daughter.

But that sort of thing was a fairly regular occurrence whenever Beth and her mother came into the store and was handled easily enough, with flustered apologies from Beth and that baffled "What did I do wrong?" look from poor Mrs. Anglesey.

She didn't think Devin would be particularly interested in that or the great commission she'd earned by selling one of the beautiful carved horses an artist friend made in the woodshop behind his house to a tourist from Maine.

And then there was the pleasant encounter with Mr. Twitchell, but she doubted that was what her sister meant.

"Sorry. You lost me somewhere. I can't think of any news I have worth sharing."

"Seriously? You didn't think I would want to know that Ben Kilpatrick is back in town?"

The knife slipped from her hands and she narrowly avoided chopping the tip of her finger off. A greasy, angry ball formed in her stomach.

Ben Kilpatrick. The only person on earth she could honestly say she despised. She picked up the knife and stabbed it through the lemon, wishing it was his cold, black heart.

"You're joking," she said, though she couldn't imagine what her sister would find remotely funny about making up something so outlandish and horrible.

"True story," Devin assured her. "I heard it from Betty Orton while I was getting gas. Apparently he strolled into the grocery store a few hours ago, casual as a Sunday morning, and bought what looked to be at least a week's worth of groceries. She said he didn't look very happy to be back. He just frowned when she welcomed him back."

"It's a mistake. That's all. She mistook him for someone else."

"That's what I said, but Betty assured me she's known him all his life and taught him in Sunday school three years in a row and she's not likely to mistake him for someone else."

"I won't believe it until I see him," she said. "He hates Haven Point. That's fairly obvious, since he's done his best to drive our town into the ground."

"Not actively," Devin, who tended to see the good in just about everyone, was quick to point out.

"What's the difference? By completely ignoring the

property he inherited after his father died, he accomplished the same thing as if he'd walked up and down Lake Street, setting a torch to the whole downtown."

She picked up the knife and started chopping the fresh tarragon with quick, angry movements. "You know how hard it's been the past five years since he inherited to keep tenants in the downtown businesses. Haven Point is dying because of one person. Ben Kilpatrick."

If she had only one goal for her next four years as mayor, she dreamed of revitalizing a town whose lifeblood was seeping away, business by business.

When she was a girl, downtown Haven Point had been bustling with activity, a magnet for everyone in town, with several gift and clothing boutiques for both men and women, restaurants and cafés, even a downtown movie theater.

She still ached when she thought of it, when she looked around at all the empty storefronts and the ramshackle buildings with peeling paint and broken shutters.

"It's his fault we've lost so many businesses and nothing has moved in to replace them. I mean, why go to all the trouble to open a business," she demanded, "if the landlord is going to be completely unresponsive and won't fix even the most basic problems?"

"You don't have to sell it to me, Kenz. I know. I went to your campaign rallies, remember?"

"Right. Sorry." It was definitely one of her hot buttons. She loved Haven Point and hated seeing its decline—much like old Mrs. Anglesey, who had once been an elegant, respected, contributing member of the community and now could barely get around even with her daughter's help and didn't remember whether she had paid for items in the store.

"It wasn't really his fault, anyway. He hired an incompetent crook of a property manager who was supposed to be taking care of things. It wasn't Ben's fault the man embezzled from him and didn't do the necessary upkeep to maintain the buildings."

"Oh, come on. Ben Kilpatrick is the chief operating officer for one of the most successful, fastest-growing companies in the world. You think he didn't know what was going on? If he had bothered to care, he would have paid more attention."

This was an argument she and Devin had had before. "At some point, you're going to have to let go," her sister said calmly. "Ben doesn't own any part of Haven Point now. He sold everything to Aidan Caine last year—which makes his presence in town even more puzzling. Why would he come back *now*, after all these years? It would seem to me, he has even *less* reason to show his face in town now."

McKenzie still wasn't buying the rumor that Ben had actually returned. He had been gone since he was seventeen years old. He didn't even come back for Joe Kilpatrick's funeral five years earlier—though she, for one, wasn't super surprised about that since Joe had been a bastard to everyone in town and especially to his only surviving child.

"It doesn't make any sense. What possible reason would he have to come back now?"

"I don't know. Maybe he's here to make amends. Did you ever think of that?"

How could he ever make amends for what he had

done to Haven Point—not to mention shattering all her girlish illusions?

Of course, she didn't mention that to Devin as she tossed the tarragon into the lemon juice while her sister continued speculating about Ben's motives for coming back to town.

Her sister probably had no idea about McKenzie's ridiculous crush on Ben, that when she was younger, she had foolishly considered him her ideal guy. Just thinking about it now made her cringe.

Yes, he had been gorgeous enough. Vivid blue eyes, long sooty eyelashes, the old clichéd chiseled jaw—not to mention that lock of sun-streaked brown hair that always seemed to be falling into his eyes, just begging for the right girl to push it back, like Belle did to the Prince after the Beast in her arms suddenly materialized into him.

Throw in that edge of pain she always sensed in him and his unending kindness and concern for his sickly younger sister and it was no wonder her thirteen-year-old self—best friends with that same sister—used to pine for him to notice her, despite the four-year difference in their ages.

It was so stupid, she didn't like admitting it, even to herself. All that had been an illusion, obviously. He might have been sweet and solicitous to Lily but that was his only redeeming quality. His actions these past five years had proved that, over and over.

Through the open kitchen window, she heard Rika start barking fiercely, probably at some poor hapless chipmunk or squirrel that dared venture into her territory.

"I'd better go," she said to Devin. "Rika's mad at something."

"Yeah, I've got to go, too. Looks like the Shelter Springs ambulance is on its way with a cardiac patient."

"Okay. Good luck. Go save a life."

Her sister was a dedicated, caring doctor at Lake Haven Hospital, as passionate about her patients as McKenzie was about their town.

"Let me know if you hear anything down at city hall about why Ben Kilpatrick has come back to our fair city after all these years."

"Sure. And then maybe you can tell me why you're so curious."

She could almost hear the shrug in Devin's voice. "Are you kidding me? It's not every day a gorgeous playboy billionaire comes to town."

And that was the crux of the matter. Somehow it seemed wholly unfair, a serious Karmic calamity, that he had done so well for himself after he left town. If she had her way, he would be living in the proverbial van down by the river—or at least in one of his own dilapidated buildings.

Rika barked again and McKenzie hurried to the back door that led onto her terrace. She really hoped it wasn't a skunk. They weren't uncommon in the area, especially not this time of year. Her dog had encountered one the week before on their morning run on a favorite mountain trail and it had taken her three baths in the magic solution she found on the internet before she could allow Rika back into the house.

Her dog wasn't in the yard, she saw immediately. Now that she was outside, she realized the barking was more excited and playful than upset. All the more reason to hope she wasn't trying to make nice with some odiferous little friend.

"Come," she called again. "Inside."

The dog bounded through a break in the bushes between the house next door, followed instantly by another dog—a beautiful German shepherd with classic markings.

She had been right. Rika *had* been making friends. She and the German shepherd looked tight as ticks, tails wagging as they raced exuberantly around the yard.

The dog must belong to the new renters of the Sloane house. Carol would pitch a royal fit if she knew they had a dog over there. McKenzie knew it was strictly prohibited.

Now what was she supposed to do?

A man suddenly walked through the gap in landscaping. He had brown hair, but a sudden piercing ray of the setting sun obscured his features more than that.

She *really* didn't want a confrontation with the man, especially not on a Friday night when she had been so looking forward to a relaxing night at home. She supposed she could just call Carole or the property management company and let them deal with the situation.

That seemed a cop-out since Carole had asked her to keep an eye on the place.

She forced a smile and approached the dog's owner. "Hi. Good evening. You must be renting the place from Carole. I'm McKenzie Shaw. I live next door. Rika, that dog you're playing catch with, is mine."

The man turned around and the pleasant evening around her seemed to go dark and still as she took in brown sun-streaked hair, steely blue eyes, chiseled jaw.

Her stomach dropped as if somebody had just picked her up and tossed her into the cold lake.

Ben Kilpatrick. Here. Staying in the house next door.

So much for her lovely evening at home.

* * * * *

Don't miss
REDEMPTION BAY by RaeAnne Thayne,
available July 2015 wherever
HQN Books are sold.
www.HQNBooks.com

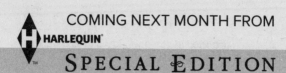

COMING NEXT MONTH FROM

HARLEQUIN®

SPECIAL EDITION

Available July 21, 2015

#2419 Do You Take This Maverick?
Montana Mavericks: What Happened at the Wedding?
by Marie Ferrarella

Claire Strickland is in mommy mode, caring for her baby girl, Bekka. She doesn't have time for nights on the town...unlike her estranged husband, Levi Wyatt. The carousing cowboy wants to prove he's man enough to keep his family together, but can he show the woman he loves that their family is truly meant to be?

#2420 One Night in Weaver...
Return to the Double C • by Allison Leigh

Psychologist Hayley Templeton has always pictured herself with an Ivy League boyfriend, but she can't seem to get sexy security guard Seth Banyon out of her mind. Overwhelmed with work, Hayley turns to Seth for relief in more ways than one. She soon finds there's more heart and passion to this seeming Average Joe than she ever could have imagined.

#2421 The Boss, the Bride & the Baby
Brighton Valley Cowboys • by Judy Duarte

Billionaire Jason Rayburn is back home on his family's Texas ranch, looking to renovate and sell off the property. So he brings in lovely Juliana Bailey to help him clean up the Leaning R. Juliana is reluctant to work with irresistibly handsome Jason, who's the son of an infamous local businessman. Besides, she has a baby secret she's trying to keep—at the risk of her heart!

#2422 The Cowboy's Secret Baby
The Mommy Club • by Karen Rose Smith

One night on a ranch, bull rider Ty Conroy gave Marissa Lopez an amazing gift—her son, Jordan. She never expected to see the freewheeling cowboy again, but Ty is back in town after a career-ending injury forced him to start over. Both Marissa and Ty are reluctant to trust one another, but doing so might just lasso them the greatest prize of all—family!

#2423 A Reunion and a Ring
Proposals & Promises • by Gina Wilkins

To ponder a proposal, Jenny Baer retreats to her childhood haunt, a cabin in the Arkansas hills. To her surprise, she's met there by her college sweetheart, ex-cop Gavin Locke. Years ago, their passion blazed brightly until Jenny convinced herself she wanted a more secure future. Can these long-lost lovers heal past wounds...and create the future together they'd always wanted?

#2424 Following Doctor's Orders
Texas Rescue • by Caro Carson

Dr. Brooke Brown works tirelessly as an ER doctor. She does her best to ignore too-handsome playboy firefighter Zach Bisho, who threatens her concentration. But not even Brooke can resist, soon succumbing to his charm, and a fling soon turns into love...even as Zach discovers his adorable long-lost daughter. Despite past hurts, Brooke and Zach soon find that there's nowhere they'd rather be than in each other's arms...forever!

YOU CAN FIND MORE INFORMATION ON UPCOMING HARLEQUIN® TITLES, FREE EXCERPTS AND MORE AT WWW.HARLEQUIN.COM.

HSECNM0715

REQUEST YOUR FREE BOOKS!
2 FREE NOVELS PLUS 2 FREE GIFTS!

H HARLEQUIN®

SPECIAL EDITION

Life, Love & Family

Claire Strickland thought she'd found The One in Levi Wyatt. But marriage and a baby put a seemingly irreparable strain on their relationship. Can Claire and Levi wrangle a true happily-ever-after with their child?

Read on for a sneak preview of
DO YOU TAKE THIS MAVERICK?
by USA TODAY bestselling author **Marie Ferrarella***,*
the second book in the 2015 Montana Mavericks continuity,
MONTANA MAVERICKS:
WHAT HAPPENED AT THE WEDDING?

"You don't mind if I see her?" he asked uncertainly.

"No, I don't mind," Claire answered in the same quiet voice. She gestured toward the baby lying in the portable playpen. "Go on, it's okay. Since Bekka lights up whenever you walk into a room, maybe it might be a good thing for her if you spent a little time with our little girl."

"Thanks," Levi said to her with feeling. Then he slanted another look toward Claire—a longer one as he tried to puzzle things out—and asked, "How do you feel about my spending time with her mother?"

Claire arched one eyebrow as she regarded him. "I wouldn't push it if I were you, Levi," she warned.

He raised his hands in a sign of complete surrender. "Message received. You don't need to say another word, Claire. My question is officially rescinded," he told her.

HSEEXP0715

And then, because he prided himself on always being truthful with Claire, he added, "I'm a patient man. I can wait until you decide to change your mind about that."

Because he had really left her no recourse if she was to save face, Claire told him, "I don't think there's enough patience in the whole world for that."

"We'll see," Levi said softly, more to himself than to her. "We'll see."

Claire gave no indication that she had overheard him. But she had.

And something very deep inside her warmed to his words.

Don't miss
DO YOU TAKE THIS MAVERICK?
by Marie Ferrarella, available August 2015 wherever
Harlequin® Special Edition books and ebooks are sold.

www.Harlequin.com

HSEEXP0715

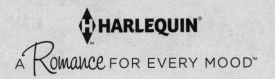

THE WORLD IS BETTER WITH

Romance

Harlequin has everything from contemporary, passionate and heartwarming to suspenseful and inspirational stories.

Whatever your mood, we have a romance just for you!

Connect with us to find your next great read, special offers and more.

f /HarlequinBooks

🐦 @HarlequinBooks

www.HarlequinBlog.com

www.Harlequin.com/Newsletters